"Striker!" Grimaldi called. "Sniper at two o'clock."

Bolan rolled into position, brought the M-16 to his shoulder and peered through the open sights. He flicked the selector to single-fire, then squeezed off six rounds.

Without warning the ground vibrations increased. A tank smashed through the rubble of a nearby shop, the machine's massive treads flattening an abandoned minivan. When the turret swung around with a whir, the Executioner knew the tank wasn't a friendly.

"Come on!" Bolan yelled, grabbing Talia by the arm and jerking her into motion. A second later the tank's 120 mm turret gun boomed.

The shell shot past the fleeing couple, but the concussion slammed them to the ground.

Bolan hit the pavement with bruising impact and heard the turret groan as it swiveled to fire another round....

MACK BOLAN®

The Executioner

DON PENDLETON'S
THE *EXECUTIONER*®
FEATURING *MACK BOLAN*®

STORM WARNING

A GOLD EAGLE BOOK FROM
W☉RLDWIDE®

TORONTO • NEW YORK • LONDON • PARIS
AMSTERDAM • STOCKHOLM • HAMBURG
ATHENS • MILAN • TOKYO • SYDNEY

First edition April 1992

ISBN 0-373-61160-9

Special thanks and acknowledgment to
Mel Odom for his contribution to this work.

STORM WARNING

Let him who desires peace prepare for war.
—Flavius Vegetius Renatus
A.D. 375

Stand your ground. Don't fire unless fired upon, but if they mean to have a war let it begin here.
—John Parker
April 19, 1775

War has a way of calling out to people when there's a need to protect hearth and home. Those who answer that call go forth into the world to face down the challenge. How many of us owe our lives to the American fighting soldier?
—Mack Bolan

To the indomitable spirit of
the American Armed Forces

PROLOGUE

Kuwait City

Billy Roy Hollister was a long way from Nacog-doches, Texas. He reflected on that while he cleaned sand from his field stripped M-16. Sitting in the middle of his bed, dressed in a T-shirt, fatigue shorts and the pair of tennis shoes that still had most of the tread on them, he kept an ear cocked for the camaraderie that pierced and echoed within the barracks room. As the top bed on the bunk, he could keep watch over the festivities without appearing obvious.

"Hey, Billy."

Hollister leaned out over the bed and looked down at his bunk mate. "What?"

Pete Cochran was sandy haired and still pink from the desert sun rather than tanned. So far he seemed to be okay for a Yankee. "You got any tobacco?"

Picking up the tin lying beside him, Hollister flashed the cap at his buddy. "Only the smokeless kind, amigo."

"Fuck that," Cochran said as he rolled off the bunk

to pull on a pair of boots. "If the sarge comes in and wants to know where I am, I'll be back in a few."

Hollister nodded as he finished reassembling the assault rifle.

It was Sunday morning in the barracks. Some of the guys were on guard duty. Others had gone to church. The rest, like him, had preferred the company inside the building as they got ready for brunch. Even as part of the United Nations peacekeeping forces assigned to Kuwait City, a wise American soldier didn't wander too far from home territory. And, all things considered, American soldiers got wise quick or they got dead.

Memories of the horror stories Hollister had been told about American soldiers getting their throats cut while out trying to photograph the city or find a Kuwaiti professional girl—surely as rare as hen's teeth, Hollister felt certain—had faded over the past two months. But he hadn't forgotten. Every two or three weeks a new victim would turn up, just enough to keep a man on his toes.

Finished with the M-16, he tapped the side of his thumb against the lid of the tobacco can, then took a pinch and put it between his cheek and gum. He pulled a leg up, put his foot on the mattress and hugged his knee.

Without warning, the front door of the barracks was thrown open and Cochran walked back in. Hollister could tell immediately that something was wrong. The soldier's steps were forced and unsteady, and his hands were wrapped around his throat. Bright bloody streamers blossomed between his fingers and ran down to soak into his T-shirt.

Sudden quiet filled the room.

Over a dozen Arabs followed Cochran into the barracks as the young Marine dropped to his knees. The lead Arab lifted a pistol and shot Cochran through the head. The body fell to the floor as the sound of the report echoed within the building.

Movement broke out all around Hollister as he reached for his M-16, his heart hammering in his chest as the swell of autofire took his hearing away. Rolling off the bed, he twisted and came around to face the advancing Arabs. The assault rifle came up to his shoulder automatically.

Cries of the wounded and the dying punctuated the din of gunfire. Cordite smoke created swirling patterns in the air.

Hollister fired at the closest Arab, saw the man go spinning away as the triburst of 5.56 mm tumblers took him in the shoulder. It was the first time he'd ever shot another human being, but the emotions involved didn't have time to sink into him because a line of bullets chewed into the wooden framework of the bed beside him. He ducked.

He stepped out to the side of the bunk bed and tried to take up a position to protect his friends. He squeezed off two more bursts, knocked down another man and swung the rifle toward the Arab leader. Even as he was putting the sights over the man's heart, he found himself looking down the barrel of the pistol in the man's hand.

For a moment he thought he could actually see the bullet coming at him as time slowed down all around him. He willed his finger to close over the M-16's trigger, then a crushing pain hammered into his chest, burying his dog tags into his flesh. A cold, still blackness blotted out his vision and carried him away.

Washington, D.C.

KAROL POLK HELD her children's hands as she listened to the young Massachusetts senator's words and uselessly fought the hot tears that burned down her cheeks. Matt, Jr., his five-year-old's face already so solemn, looked up at her and squeezed her hand. He looked so grown-up in his suit.

"Don't cry, Mommie. Daddy never liked to see you cry. You don't want him to see you crying now."

Her heart wanted to break at his words. He'd been so quiet around her these past few days when the hurting had started again, but she'd heard him taking his own grief out in his room when he thought no one was listening.

"Be quiet, Matt," Elizabeth hissed from Karol's other side. She was four years older, so prim and proper in her black dress.

With an effort Karol stilled her tears and lifted her head, focusing on the black marble slab in front of them that had drawn the families together a year af-

ter the official end of the war. Although she couldn't
read Richard's name, she knew from memory where
it was and how it read: Sgt. Richard T. Polk, Yuma,
AZ USMC.

"This was meant to be a day for honoring our war
dead," the senator said in his clear voice. "But it
seems we're in store for more sorrows yet to come. As
you know from today's news broadcasts, an American contingent of the United Nations peacekeeping
forces was attacked almost twelve hours ago by unknown Arab terrorists. So far there have been in ex-
cess of eighty casualties. Forty-three of those are dead.
Another twenty or more have been taken captive. At
this point the Pentagon is uncertain where they are
being held. Rest assured we're doing everything possible to ensure their safe return."

The old woman next to Karol bowed her head,
crossed herself and began praying in a dry voice. Beyond her, Karol watched as another news van pulled
to a stop at the curb beside the memorial garden area.
A part of her mind said the late arrival of the news
team was unusual. During the past year she'd noted
that media people tended to arrive early in anticipation of the ghoulish parade of events about to unfold,
then depart once they were certain every morsel of
flesh had been stripped from the bones.

The news crew took their time about getting out.

Farther down from them stood three men Karol had
noticed earlier. A tall blond man leaned against some
sort of off-road vehicle beside a Hispanic man and a

gray-haired man. Because of her long association with Richard—and through him, the Marine Corps—she was certain the men were military. Or had been at one time.

"If you'll bow your heads," the senator said, "I'd like you all to join me in a quiet moment of prayer for the loved ones we lost a year ago, and the ones we've lost only today."

Karol bowed her head and wished she could see past her loss to something she could hang on to for a future.

The rasp of the news van's door swinging open behind the crowd was unnaturally loud.

"Mommie," Matt, Jr., yelled, "those men have guns!"

Alarmed, Karol glanced over her shoulder as other cries of warning rippled through the crowd.

Over a dozen men had leaped from the van and landed in the middle of the flower beds surrounding the dedication site. Multicolored flowers went down under their booted feet as they spread out. The hard and angular weapons in their hands were unfamiliar to Karol, yet the harsh rattle of the guns was familiar enough.

Men and women fell in waves under the bullets. Blood splattered against Karol's face as she dragged her two children to the ground and pulled them close to her. Everyone standing or running was a target. She knew that.

She twisted her head, turned to look at the Marine honor guard, willed them to do something.

Instead, she saw that half of them had already been killed or wounded. The survivors were scrambling for position and fumbling in their pockets. She realized with a sinking sensation in the pit of her stomach that the magazines in their M-16s held only blanks for their part in the dedication ceremony.

"Death to the Americans!" one of the men shouted as he fired his weapon into the bodies littering the ground. "God will give us the strength we need to fight the American Satans! The Arab people *will* be free!"

A few of the Marines had managed to load their weapons and were returning fire. But it was too little, too late.

Karol tucked her children in close to her as the Arab terrorists took cover from the Marines' bullets. Two of their attackers were down. Another was shouldering a long tube, aiming it at the Persian Gulf War Memorial. There was a whoosh, and a puff of white smoke belched from the end of the tube.

Then a crack of thunder ripped loose.

Karol saw the black slab bearing her husband's name disintegrate into thousands of pieces of flying rock. She held her children and turned her head into the ground as fear consumed her.

1

Full dark was just settling over the streets when Mack Bolan rolled into Kuwait City. Klaxons screamed intermittently, their strident wails rising and falling as emergency rescue vehicles threaded through the piles of rubble and wreckage that remained from the war a year earlier. Fighter jets ran patterns over the city ceaselessly as two dragonfly-shaped HueyCobra AH-1Ss skimmed the lower levels.

The Executioner steered the battered Land Rover to the far side of the street while he scanned the war zone through the bug-spattered and dust-caked windshield. He kept the door windows down so his hearing wouldn't be blocked by the glass. The dashboard instrument lights had been carefully cut shortly after he'd bought the vehicle so the shadows inside would remain complete.

Bolan was outfitted in dark clothes and boots. Only his brown bomber jacket reflected any kind of light. His Beretta 93-R rode in shoulder leather, and a Cold Steel Tanto fighting knife was sheathed in his boot. A 35 mm camera, pocket tape recorder and a fistful of spiral-bound notebooks occupied the passenger seat as part of his cover ID.

In the distance tongues of fire leaped toward the sky over the American portion of the UN peace force headquarters, followed by gray wreaths of smoke.

He made a right turn, and his headlights swept over the military unit checkpoint down the street. The uniforms were British army under the blue helmets designating the UN peace forces.

He braked when a sergeant waved him to a halt. The Heckler & Koch MP-5 canted on the soldier's hip lowered almost imperceptibly to the point where it could be dropped into target acquisition and brought into use immediately. The military flap over the Browning Hi-Power holstered on his hip had been tied back to leave the weapon ready for instant use.

A corporal drifted into position along the passenger side of the Land Rover as the sergeant approached.

Bolan held his hands palm-up against the glare of the sergeant's flashlight splashing across the dirty windshield.

"Good evening, sir," the sergeant said in a clipped British accent. "I'm afraid I'm going to have to trouble you for a look at your papers."

"I hear you people went under some heavy fire," Bolan said as he reached carefully under his jacket and produced his papers.

"We seem to have a lock on it now." The sergeant tucked his flashlight under his free arm, then leaned in to accept the papers. "The American chaps appear to have caught the brunt of the attack."

"How bad is the casualty list?"

"I'm afraid I can't go into that. It says here that you're a reporter, Mr. McKay."

"I try to be." Bolan gave the guy a grin he didn't feel. More than fifty American soldiers were confirmed dead now, and the total missing had been upped to nearly forty. The time it had taken to work through the security that had been clamped down on the city after the attack and the bombing chafed at him. "But it's hard to be any good at it when I keep getting stonewalled everywhere I go."

The sergeant closed the papers with a snap, then presented them back. "I think the military liaison's office for you Americans is scheduled to begin in one of the downtown motels in half an hour. If you hurry, you might make the beginning."

"I'd heard about it," Bolan replied as he put the papers away, "but the briefing is being held nowhere near the attack site."

"Yes, well, that's how it is, you see. I'm afraid no unauthorized personnel are being permitted past this point for now."

"And news people are unauthorized?"

"Definitely. I'm going to have to ask you to turn your vehicle around and head back the way you came, Mr. McKay. And you have a good evening."

"Thank you, Sergeant." Bolan shoved the gear shift into reverse. The transmission whined, and the headlights pulled away to let the blockade melt back into the night.

Bolan cut the wheel, straightened out and slipped his map case from the jumble of reporter's things in the passenger seat. He flipped it open as he parked three blocks down, then played his penlight over the Kuwait City street map.

His eyes felt grainy and stung as he traced the side streets with a forefinger. He'd been on the go for most of the past twenty-four hours with only catnaps to fight off the fatigue. Even with the cybernetic feelers spread out from Stony Man Farm and the fuzzy warnings Aaron Kurtzman's teams had picked up concerning possible terrorist activity, he'd started out hours behind the terrorists. Hard work had maybe cut that to minutes, but it remained to be seen.

After memorizing the information he needed and sending a hopeful prayer winging into the night that most of the street signs remained intact, the warrior put the map away and let out the clutch.

Ten minutes later he found a suitable spot for the Land Rover in a dead-end alley. He parked it in the shadows, nose turned toward the street. He got out, shrugged free of the bomber jacket, threw it onto the seat, then locked the doors.

He dropped and rolled under the 4X4. He retrieved a canvas-wrapped Mossberg Bullpup 12 from the front bumper, then took a Walther MPK Model S from along the drive-shaft housing. Military webbing containing extra magazines for all his weapons, and other munitions came from the rear fender-walls. The Israeli Desert Eagle .44 was tucked in beside the Rover's gas tank.

The warrior slid into his gear as he moved out. The Mossberg shotgun was slung down his back over the military webbing so the buttstock was within quick reach of his right hand. The Desert Eagle rode on his right hip. He carried the Walther submachine gun up and ready.

Although Kurtzman hadn't been able to turn up any hard information on who had fielded the Arab terrorists or where the missing American soldiers were being held, he'd uncovered a man in Stony Man files who might know.

The Executioner passed unseen through the night. There were UN peace force foot patrols laying down perimeters, as well as jeep-mounted mobile units. The numbers counting down his present operation whispered like quicksilver through his mind. His primary objective was to find and free the American soldiers. Intel led the Stony Man teams and Military Intelligence to believe they were being held somewhere within the city.

The secondary purpose of the probe was to establish who had instigated the attack and if it was going to be repeated.

Bolan's own suspicions were that the initial attack against the American barracks was only the tip of the iceberg.

He found the building without trouble, had to wait a moment as a collection of Kuwaiti and American soldiers passed, then silently drifted through the entrance. The inside of the building was dark on both stories. He went up the creaky stairs with his elbow guiding him along the wall. From the state of the structure, he figured it wasn't just the threat of another attack that kept the lights off.

Blinded by the total darkness of the hallway, he used his fingertips against the unseen metal numbers nailed to the doors. The one he searched for had a number missing, but checking the door farther on left no options, so he went back.

Bolan lifted the Walther MPK, then rapped sharply on the door. He stepped to one side as a voice called out in a questioning tone. The warrior murmured indistinguishable words deep in his throat that were meant to sound authoritative and urgent.

Footsteps shushed across the wooden floor and approached the door. A shadow cut the thin yellow line of light peeping out from under the door's edge, then blotted it out completely.

Bolan rapped his knuckles forcefully against the door once more.

Two sliding bolts snicked back, and the door opened.

Holding the little Walther at the ready in one hand, the Executioner kicked the man who'd opened the door in the crotch, then used his free hand to push the guy away. His breath taken by the numbing pain of the blow, the man dropped to the floor as if he'd been poleaxed and remained there.

Three other men were in the room, sitting around a table with cards and money spread across its top. One of them made to move toward the holstered revolver hanging from the back of his chair.

Bolan motioned with the submachine gun. "That wouldn't be the wisest thing you've done today," he said in a graveyard voice.

The man reluctantly sat back down.

"I want Hamal Ghinzarli."

Two of the men pointed at the third while that man glared at his companions.

"Get up," Bolan commanded.

Ghinzarli held his hands up and spoke Arabic.

"You speak English," the warrior said. "I've seen paper on you. Get up and get over here or they'll be able to close the file on you after tonight."

Reluctantly the man did as he was told.

The groaning man on the floor climbed to his knees.

Bolan froze the guy into place with the ugly snout of the Walther. "Over there. Slowly." He waved slightly with the submachine gun, indicating the other two card players sitting at the table.

The man crept to the table and sat in a chair that squeaked under his impressive weight.

"Hands on your head," Bolan told Ghinzarli as the man stopped just short of arm's reach. Once the Arab had his hands on his head, the Executioner went through a quick one-handed frisk that turned up a small Webley automatic and a pair of curved knives. He tossed the collection of weapons onto the sway-backed bed in the corner of the small room. Taking down one of the Arab's arms, the warrior grabbed the wrist and tucked it up securely between the man's shoulder blades. He guided him to the door, keeping the Walther trained on the three men at the table.

They went down the stairs together.

Bolan used his captive as a shield from an attack coming from the front of the building while keeping the submachine gun between himself and the three men who trailed behind them at a discreet distance. Hard metal glinted in the trio's hands.

The Executioner knew the men wouldn't let them pass unchallenged. He could tell from the way Ghinzarli tensed as they neared the door that the man knew it, too.

The guy who'd been kicked was the first to move. He raised a large-bore revolver that spit a full foot of muzzle flame, the thunder crack of the report filling the enclosed space of the building.

The Executioner squeezed off a 3-round burst that scored across the big man's chest and toppled him over the railing, the wooden flooring breaking under the impact of the corpse.

A bullet from one of the other men's guns dug a crater in the plaster wall beside Bolan's head.

The warrior released Ghinzarli and pushed him through the door as he took a two-handed grip on the Walther and burned through what remained of the 32-

round clip. The bullets started at ankle level through the wooden spokes of the bannister railing as he swept the weapon across his opponents, and rose to throat high as he stitched a figure eight.

The two men were driven back by the hail of bullets, crimson smearing the walls behind them as their bodies slumped to the hallway floor.

Bolan changed magazines and raced after Ghinzarli. The informant was making good time all on his own. The Executioner grabbed him by the back of his robe and redirected the man's flight.

Behind them pursuit was already being organized, and Bolan figured at least a handful of people had been watching their escape from the building. A Klaxon shrilled as a military vehicle vectored in on the area.

"You keep running," Bolan growled into his prisoner's ear, "and you run where I tell you to. If I pass you, I'm leaving a dead man behind me. Understand?"

The Arab nodded vigorously and put more effort into his stride.

As a Kuwaiti jeep wheeled around the far corner behind them, Bolan yanked Ghinzarli into an alley.

CARL LYONS THREW himself to the ground as a burst of autofire speared through the air above his head. His ears still rang from the LAW-80 round that had detonated against the Persian Gulf War Memorial. Bits of black marble continued to rain down all around him and slam against his body.

He rolled as he clawed the .357 Colt Python from shoulder leather under his windbreaker. Another line of 5.56 mm tumblers chopped through immaculate lawn and flowers. Blades of grass and brightly colored blossoms spilled over the Able Team warrior as he leveled the big revolver in front of him. Placing the target sights over one of the terrorists' hearts, he squeezed the trigger through double-action. It bucked in his fist, and the terrorist went over backward.

At least two rounds thudded into his back and the Kevlar body armor he wore. The bullets flattened out and ricocheted away.

"Ironman!"

It was Hermann Schwarz, bellowing into his ear through the ear-throat radio.

"I'm okay." Lyons pushed himself up and pointed the .357 Magnum at a terrorist firing from behind the edge of the news van. Four hollowpoint rounds ripping through the sheet metal convinced the shooter that his position wasn't as defensible as he'd thought. The Arab dropped from view. "Politician."

"Yeah, amigo," Rosario Blancanales answered.

Lyons fired his final round into a terrorist's exposed thigh as the guy crouched behind one of the six decorative stone pillars surrounding the outer perimeter of the war memorial site. The terrorist came spinning out into the open for a moment, and Lyons regretted instantly that he didn't have a follow-up shot ready before the man had time to crawl back to safety. "You got a clear view of the situation?"

"Yes."

Lyons whirled into place behind one of the oak trees left carefully spaced in the landscape. He dumped out the empty casings, dug a speedloader from his pocket and quickly inserted a fresh load. "How many men?"

"I count nine left standing."

"That's what I get," Schwarz said. "How many did you see?" Lyons flipped the cylinder back and thumbed back the hammer. "I didn't. I've been kind of busy here if you hadn't noticed. These guys have been trained to shoot at the biggest guy first."

He peeked out around the tree and took a swift head count. All of the Marine honor guard were down now. Blood spattered the dress uniforms, showing dramatically against the white gloves and caps. He couldn't begin to guess how many civilians were down. He didn't let himself think about the wounded children. If he had, he'd have lost the thin veneer of control left to him.

Lyons had been a street cop in L.A. for a lot of years before joining Able Team. He'd seen his share of desperation and despair, and he'd seen the remains of people who'd been pushed too far. The images of fathers who'd killed their whole families rather than lose them to failing economics had always left a sourness in his stomach that sometimes took weeks to fade into something he could bear. That same feeling of helplessness filled him now.

Even if they were able to put every member of the attacking terrorist team down, they still lost.

One of the Arabs raced from his position, tried to close in on the knots of shouting and crying people fleeing into the sparse forest the landscapers had allowed to remain in the park area.

Lyons braced his wrist on his forearm and squeezed the trigger. The .357 boomed. The terrorist went down as the hollowpoint blew away half of his head.

A fresh wave of autofire chewed into the tree where Lyons stood. Jacketed lead talons scraped away the bark and left the scarred white flesh of the oak exposed.

"Looks like Barb's Intel was on the money," Lyons said grimly. He reached behind his back with his other hand and freed the Colt .45 Government Model from his waistband.

"It's too bad she and Kurtzman couldn't get enough solid information to allow us to take these bastards out before they made their play," Schwarz said.

Lyons spotted his teammate streaking for cover closer to the action. Schwarz was lean and gray-haired, his skin tanned and weathered from battles he'd seen in a lot of hot spots. The beginning had been in Vietnam with Mack Bolan during PenTeam Able's war against the NVA. Since then, he'd returned to the Executioner's fold with Able Team, the domestic arm of the Stony Man Farm operation. When it came to mechanical or electronic devices that could be used for booby traps, surveillance or nasty surprises in general, he was a master. He'd earned the nicknames of "Gadgets" and "Wizard" dozens of times over.

"So now we make up for lost time," Blancanales stated flatly. He added the chatter of his CAR-15 to the basso boom of Lyons' .357, using the armored bulk of the full-size Bronco 4x4 for cover. Like Schwarz, he'd been a member of PenTeam Able. Hispanic and stocky, with a mustache, Blancanales was a fierce fighter who could get down and dirty in the trenches. Yet his nickname of "Politician" reflected the gift he had for handling people and volatile situations that didn't have to go ballistic. When, as today's battle proved, there was no peaceful way out, he was a deadly enemy.

Two of the terrorists turned to meet Schwarz's advance, the muzzles of their M-16s coming onto line.

"Gadgets," Lyons roared as he keyed his radio to life, "grab some turf!"

Schwarz went down into a slide face-first that brought him into rough contact with a three-foot-high stone pillar.

Lyons fired the Government .45 left-handed, snapping off three rounds that caught one of the terrorists in the chest and punched him to the ground. He heard the flat crack of Blancanales's CAR-15 on single-shot, then a red flower blossomed between the other terrorist's eyes as his head jerked back.

That made three down the way Lyons had it counted. He scanned for the other six as he reloaded the .357.

A whirling buzz saw of noise echoed from overhead.

Lyons looked up and saw a news copter hovering over the area. He hit the transmit button on his earthroat communications rig. "Politician."

"Go."

"You see the flyboy?"

"Couldn't miss him."

"Neither can those terrorists. You've got the radio inside the Bronco. Those news guys are probably monitoring the police band. See if you can get hold of the pilot and tell him to haul his ass out of here."

"You and Gadgets—"

"Will be just fine," Schwarz cut in.

Blancanales dropped back to the front of the Bronco. A bullet starred the bulletproof glass in the driver's door as he opened it and disappeared inside.

Using a Weaver's stance, Lyons finished the clip in the .45 in rapid fire and drove the remaining terrorists into cover. "Gadgets."

"Yo."

"Cover me."

"I'm on it."

Reloaded now, Lyons cut around the tree and exploded into a broken-field run between the trees that closed the distance between himself and the blasted war monument. Some of the civilians were still moving. The ones left alive, whether wounded or simply too frightened to move, would be easy targets for the terrorists. And, judging the attack to be a written lesson for whatever message the terrorists intended, the killers wouldn't rest until they crossed every *T* and dotted every *I*. Lyons hoped to raise the ante to something that would be too costly for the terrorists to continue the attack.

"Down, Carl!" Gadgets ordered.

Lyons went to ground, barely catching the movement on his periphery, and rolled onto his back as the sharp crack of Schwarz's assault rifle belched out a 3-round burst. He saw the leaping terrorist stiffen in midair, then the corpse slammed into Lyons with enough force to take his breath away.

He kicked the body off and pushed back into his forward momentum as terrorist bullets raked the ground where he'd been. He fell into position behind another tree and gazed out over the twisted bodies in front of the shattered monument.

Some had been killed by the concussion of the blast. Others had been ripped and torn by the flying debris. Arms and legs lay scattered and separated from their original bodies.

To Lyons it looked like a small garden corner of Hell. And there was no way the seeds sown today wouldn't bear bitter fruit.

The hit squad suddenly seemed of two minds. A pair of the surviving members rushed for the body of the man Lyons had downed in the beginning moments of the battle. The expended LAW launcher lay only inches from the terrorist's outstretched fingers.

Now, from his new position, Lyons could see at least two more of the deadly tubes poking out of the cloth satchel hanging across the dead man's back.

The other two terrorists were clambering back aboard the news van.

Lyons hit the transmit button on his headset. "Look alive, guys. The two men still on the ground are diving for at least a pair of rocket launchers on the guy I dropped."

Blancanales and Schwarz let bullets be their answer. But from their positions they couldn't get a straight shot at their targets.

Targeting the lead man as he dived for the corpse, Lyons squeezed off a round from the .45.

The bullet smashed into the terrorist's shoulder and deflected him for a moment.

Before Lyons could follow up with another shot, a solid burst from the second terrorist's assault rifle drove him to cover. He caught a glimpse of the first man's bloody fingers closing over one of the LAW tubes. The big man cursed vehemently as he put the .45 away and took the .357 up in both hands.

He waited until the terrorist's magazine ran dry, then whirled around the tree and dropped the revolver into target acquisition. Only a portion of the terrorist's back was exposed as the guy readied the rocket launcher. Lyons sent two shots speeding into the palm-sized area.

The terrorist jerked under the impacts, but Lyons could tell neither had cored through a lung as he'd hoped. The angle was all wrong for that.

The Able Team warrior reluctantly took cover again as the terrorist with the assault rifle came back on-line. Splinters from the bark ripped into the flesh of his forearms when he brought them around.

He peered around the tree only to be forced back by a 3-round burst that scattered hunks of bark across his face. Lyons thumbed back the Python's hammer. He knew he might have only the one shot left and didn't want it to be with double-action.

"He's yours, Ironman," Blancanales transmitted. "The guy with the rifle is down."

Without hesitation, working on the trust that had served to keep the three of them alive during the deadliest of encounters, Lyons wheeled around and locked onto his target with both elbows bent. He aimed for the guy's eye sighting down the rocket launcher.

He fired.

And he saw the jet of gray smoke puff from the rear of the LAW that let him know his shot had been a heartbeat too late.

The hollowpoint caught the terrorist above the eye, split the eyebrow neatly, then took away most of the other side of his head. The body crumpled to the ground as the rocket crashed into the helicopter overhead.

The news helicopter blew apart. Lyons had a brief impression of the main rotor blowing free, then the craft popped like a Plexiglass-and-metal bubble. A ball of flame tried to swallow the debris before it could come hurtling into the ground below. It failed, and metal rain pinged from trees and the stone pillars or smacked into the ground.

Lyons's attention switched to the news van as it roared away from the curb. He fired at the tires but missed as the driver took evasive action.

A pair of Washington, D.C., police cars rolled into view at the end of the street as Lyons ran for the fallen terrorist and the remaining LAW 80.

Out on the street the police cars skidded sideways within yards of each other and blocked the traffic. The news van cut a big U-turn, the outside front tire bumping over the curbs on both sides of the street. It came around wobbling. Black smoke belched from the tailpipe as the driver tromped the accelerator again.

Lyons snatched the rocket launcher and sprinted for the street. He freed the extensions on the LAW automatically, his attention on the van as it roared down on him. He came to a halt in the middle of the street, flipped up the sights and settled the weapon onto his shoulder. He bracketed the flat nose of the van.

The passenger side of the windshield suddenly exploded, and the snout of an assault rifle poked through the opening. Three-round bursts swept across the pavement as the gunner searched for the range. Bits of concrete stung Lyons's ankles.

There was no hesitation in the big Able Team warrior as he tightened his finger on the LAW's trigger. He'd dealt with Arab terrorists before. They gave no quarter in their battles, and didn't understand it when it was offered. Their devotion to their cause was unquestioned by any counterterrorist group that had crossed swords with them. Trying to take these men alive would cost lives, and Lyons refused to put any more on the line.

The 94 mm warhead leaped from the rocket launcher, a streamer of gray-white smoke trailing in to detonation against the van's grille. The resulting explosion lifted the vehicle's roof up and peeled it back like the lid on a sardine can while showering liquid fire over the passengers. Out of control and deflected by the expended force of the rocket, the burning vehicle bounded up over the curb on the opposite side of the war memorial site. It came to a dead stop against a light pole.

Lyons tossed the useless LAW to the ground. Six more patrol cars had screeched onto the scene, and a ring of armed policemen surrounded them. He glanced at his teammates.

Blancanales was helping a woman with a small daughter and an even smaller son to their feet. The woman checked her children, then quickly pulled their faces into the folds of her dress to take their eyes from the dead lying around them.

Down on one knee, Schwarz was examining a cluster of terrorists.

Reaching inside his windbreaker, Lyons pulled out the Justice Department credentials Barbara Price and Aaron Kurtzman had fixed for them. "Agent Lewis," he said in a loud voice. "I'm with Justice. We're in charge here. Call SOG chief Harold Brognola for confirmation."

A police sergeant reached inside his car and pulled out the microphone.

The burning van gave out a series of short and sharp explosions, crackling as it continued to burn.

In the back of the line of police cars blocking the east end of the street, an unmarked sedan pulled to a rocking stop. Two undercover cops got out and worked through the line of uniforms.

"Ironman."

Lyons turned at the sound of Schwarz's voice. Already the surviving media people were picking up their abandoned cameras. He found himself looking at a growing line of camcorders and 35 mm cameras. He touched the transmit button on the throat-ear headset. "What?"

Schwarz gestured toward the body of a terrorist in front of him. "We got a live one here."

For a brief flickering moment, Lyons didn't know whether to be disappointed that they hadn't gotten them all the first time, or glad the trail leading back to the terrorists hadn't abruptly ended. He put his emotions aside and concentrated on his cop sense. They had a lead in the making. For now, it would have to be enough

"Hal?"

"Yes, Mr. President." Harold Brognola turned off the electric razor and put it on the dining room table. He dodged past two federal marshals helping to ferry suitcases out of his house, then grabbed the yellow legal pad from the table and thumbed a ballpoint pen into action.

He peeked into the kitchen to check on his wife. Helen was a godsend. She always had been. But back in the early days of their marriage, he hadn't always been able to see that. Even now, with hell breaking out all around them, Helen was able to shift gears smoothly and get everything organized around him. She and Joan Meredith, another Justice agent, were in the kitchen boxing up perishable foodstuffs to donate to one of the shelters for the homeless.

With things going on as they were, Brognola wasn't sure when they'd be returning to the house. The President had already put him in charge of the covert arm going into action against the unknown Arab terrorist faction. Despite the secrecy involved, he'd learned a long time back that word got around quickly. And he had no intention of leaving either himself or Helen exposed to any kind of terrorist retaliation.

The usual calls had been made, with each of them sharing the burden. Their children would quietly fade out of sight for a few days and be assigned Secret Service agents to protect them. The mail would be delayed, and a phone service would be picking up domestic calls.

"Are you aware of the attack that just went down at the Persian Gulf War Memorial site?" the Man asked.

"Yes, sir. Able is covering that now. From the last word I received from Lyons, they're accompanying a surviving terrorist to Walter Reed Hospital. They think he's going to make it."

"Do any of the press know about this?"

"Not yet. We're keeping it under wraps. Lyons was thinking on his feet and had the terrorist shipped out with some of the other civilian survivors. As far as the media knows at this point, all the terrorists were killed."

"Able is keeping a close watch on this man?"

"Yes." Brognola saw Helen and Meredith come from the kitchen, read his wife's lips as she mouthed the words, "I'm ready." He nodded.

The President gave a heartfelt sigh. "Maybe it'll give us something to work on."

"That's what we're hoping."

"I suppose there's no chance of ferrying the wounded terrorist to Stony Man Farm and the medical facilities there?"

"No, sir. We know he'll make it to Walter Reed, but maybe not much farther."

"I'd feel better if we could close this guy off from the outside world completely."

"So would I, but you take what you can get."

"Yeah. Any word from our man in Kuwait?"

"No. He should have been in-country for something short of an hour by now. When he knows anything, we'll know it."

The President paused for a moment.

Brognola watched as Helen got the last of their needed personal things out of the house. He took a last look around. His home, even though it hadn't insulated him from the pressures and stresses of his job, had always provided outlets of different sorts. There were the carpentry and plumbing jobs that seemed to come along on a fairly regular basis, the flower beds and the small vegetable garden in back. It was his home, and it never felt more like it than when he had to leave it. He couldn't help wondering when, and if, he'd be able to get back to it.

"A number of people said I made the decision to pull us out of the Iraqi conflict too early," the President said. "With this happening, even though we haven't pinpointed the home base for these people, I can't help but think maybe I was too premature."

"Hindsight's twenty-twenty, Mr. President," Brognola replied. "Umpires' and referees' jobs got a lot easier when the instant video-replays were allowed into the games. With a political situation, you don't see the end result of a play or strategy for months and sometimes years."

"I thought after Hussein abdicated for parts unknown, we might have a change in thinking over in that part of the world. Instead, Khalid Shawiyya has proved an even more tenacious enemy. He hasn't made any overt moves against us or our allies.''

"Until," Brognola said, "perhaps now."

"Perhaps," the Man agreed. "But I can't help but feel an ill wind is going to blow Desert Storm back over this country. And I'm not sure if anyone's ready for the long and drawn-out affair this is promising to be."

Brognola silently agreed.

"I'm pushing paperwork through the Joint Chiefs of Staff this afternoon," the President went on. "I want your teams on this in a tactical capacity. Whatever you people need, you'll have it. Make this thing go away, Hal, before it gets any worse."

"We'll do our best, sir."

"Godspeed, my friend." The President broke the connection.

Brognola looked around the dining room, kitchen and living room one last time. Helen waited patiently by the door. He dropped his snub-nosed .38 into his jacket pocket, touched the two speedloaders in his other pocket and bumped an elbow against the Colt Delta Elite 10 mm leathered on his hip.

He and Helen were guided into the waiting armor-plated limousine at almost a dead run. He slid into the rear seat with his wife. Two men rode up front.

"I don't know when I'm going to see you again," Brognola said to his wife.

A small, mischievous smile played across her lips. Her hand covered a small control panel built into the door. An electronic hum sounded as dark glass slid up and shut away the front of the limousine. "Then let's make the most of it, my love."

Brognola filled his arms with her and held her tight. He hugged her fiercely, her breath warm in his ear.

"You must come home to me when this is over," Helen said.

He kept silent as he held her. He didn't make promises he wasn't sure he could keep, and she knew it.

2

An easterly breeze blew in from the Mediterranean Sea and swept across the tree-lined Ramblas promenade in Barcelona. The sun was sliding slowly into a gathering bank of storm clouds to the west, and the last few rays touched up the flowers in the vendors' stalls with fresh color.

Yakov Katzenelenbogen dipped his head only for a moment as he ignited a filterless Camel cigarette. He spit out a fleck of tobacco and watched the roving bands of U.S. athletes gathered in Spain for the summer Olympic Games. There were Olympic hopefuls in the promenade from other countries, as well, and all were dressed as the Americans in color schemes reflecting the flags of their nations.

Dark-skinned Spanish guardsmen armed with pistols, rifles and badges of office roamed the packed promenade with grim authority. Their peaked caps set them apart at a glance. The news was only now breaking about the terrorist attack on American soil. Katz had overheard a group of Frenchmen wondering what the United States President would do to exact vengeance. They didn't know the hunt for vengeance had already begun, but the objective was prevention rather than retaliation. So far.

The earpiece of Katz's throat-ear headset buzzed for attention. He pulled the mouthpiece down from his close-cropped gray hair and covered it with the palm of his artificial right hand. "Go," he said softly.

"Hey, mate," David McCarter's voice said, "we might have a spot of trouble headed our way. From what Rafael was able to pick up from the Spanish coast guard, four helicopters have just left the deck of a Jordanian transport ship."

Katz's eyes immediately swept the twilight skies overhead. "Where is the ship bound for?"

"Marseilles, to off-load a shipment of potash."

"And her last port of call?"

There was a muffled conversation just below the range of Katz's hearing.

The Phoenix Force leader estimated the number of American athletes drifting through the promenade. The trip through the Ramblas had been given low-key publicity. The populace of many countries might not have even known of it. But, if all was as Barbara Price's and Aaron Kurtzman's findings had led them to believe, the Arab terrorists were aware of the planned visit. A cold, hard knot formed in Katz's stomach. He remembered the murders of the Israeli athletes in Munich during the Olympic Games of 1972 all too well. And the handpicked team Golda Meir had fielded to find their murderers had been associates of his.

McCarter returned in short order. "Had to run a query through Stony Man from the computer linkup. The Spaniards haven't a clue yet. From what the Bear says, the Jordanian freighter *House of Naif* departed Tripoli, Libya, more than a week ago."

"That's too much time for a shipping vessel to be en route. Time is money in that business." Katz drew a small pair of binoculars from inside his jacket and strode from the street toward one of the multistoried houses lining both sides of the promenade.

"Not to mention being this close to Barcelona takes those lads a wee bit off course for Marseilles." McCarter's clipped voice left little doubt of the dark thoughts that were sifting through his mind. The man was ex-SAS and had been blooded through his experiences in efforts against terrorism. "And there's the interesting fact that Khaddafi outfits a number of terrorist organizations willing to attack the United States."

Katz's own days with the Israeli military and in his tenure with the Mossad were sending too many possible scenarios through his mind. None of them were pleasant. "Any ID on the helicopters?" He stepped onto the wooden stairs leading up to the top of a four-storied building. Holding his hand over the Beretta 92-F sheathed under his right arm, he took the steps two and three at a time.

"Small and fast," McCarter radioed back. "They dropped below radar range within minutes of their departure."

Katz rounded the deck leading to the third-floor stairs. A few of the Spanish policemen had noted him now and were trailing in fleet-footed pursuit. The promenade's visitors eddied about in increasing consternation.

Tapping the transmit button as he gained the last stairs leading to the roof of the building, Katz said, "Manning. James."

"Here," Calvin James responded.

"Me too," Gary Manning answered.

"We're assuming hostile intentions on the part of the four helicopters. You people have the rooftops." Katz threw a leg over the low railing running around the roof and clambered over. "I'm joining you. Whenever you feel you can safely eliminate any of the crews aboard those craft, do so."

"Roger," James said. He was an ex-Navy SEAL and was skilled in the use of the M-21 Beretta sniper rifle he carried, as well as an assortment of deadly weapons Phoenix Force had found need of.

"Understood." Manning clicked out. The only one of the team who didn't have previous military experience, the big Canadian was nevertheless a decidedly deadly foe. He had a sure and brutally efficient hand with a virtual smorgasbord of explosives.

"McCarter?"

"Yes."

"Have Rafael radio our Spanish contacts and give them the information we've received. Have them get the street police to start evacuating the promenade."

"Affirmative, mate. After that I'll be joining you."

"You'll be more than welcome, my friend." Katz recovered the briefcase he'd hidden under the bulky air-conditioning unit after arriving at the promenade. Inside was a Beretta M-21 sniper rifle with a Tasco scope. Despite the prosthesis, he snapped the weapon together in seconds and slammed the first of five clips into it as he went to stand by the railing overlooking the east end of the Ramblas.

People stared up at him.

The eastern sky stayed empty. He knew the twilight would favor the approaching helicopters. If they ran dark, they wouldn't even be silhouettes against the horizon.

"You will hold it right there, *señor*," a harsh voice said.

Katz carefully put the rifle down, canted against the railing. He raised his hands and turned slowly.

The Spanish policeman held a 9 mm Super Star in a gloved fist. Another man passed him when he waved the second man forward. When the second man had taken up a stance, the first man climbed onto the rooftop.

"There is a paper in my pocket you need to see," Katz said in a calm voice. "It is signed by the Council of Ministers and the Cortes. You've been briefed concerning the presence of Operation Shadow Fox?"

The first policeman gestured to the second. "Carlo, search this man. Find out if what he says is true."

Katz offered no resistance as the second man forced him down to his knees, then removed the 9 mm Beretta and the contents of his jacket pockets.

Carlo handed the sergeant the vinyl-clad document. The sergeant read it briefly.

Evidently the document carried the necessary weight. The police sergeant snapped it closed and returned it. He hostered his pistol, then gave orders for Carlo to return Katz's weapon.

The slap of leather on wood came from the stairway, and McCarter's head bobbed into view a few heartbeats later. The fox-faced Briton jumped over the railing easily, despite the obviously heavy pack strapped across his shoulder. Dressed in street clothes and yellow-tinted aviator glasses, the lanky Phoenix Force warrior looked like an urban guerrilla carrying his Steyr AUG. A Browning Hi-Power rode on his hip, covered by a low-cut light field jacket.

Glancing over the railing of the building, Katz saw mounted policemen shouting at the gathering of Olympic athletes and waving them off the street and away from the promenade grounds. The horses looked like small, furred kayaks braving an ocean of people.

"Had me an idea once I cut loose from Rafael," McCarter explained when he dug both hands into the zippered mouth of the pack. "How's your pitching arm?" He showed Katz a spherical AN-M8 smoke grenade. "Way I figure it, those bastards will have a bloody time of it trying to hit something they can't see."

"Agreed." Katz accepted a half dozen of the grenades and lined them up perfunctorily across the railing.

"They'll buy us a couple minutes," McCarter said. He passed the rest of them out between himself and the two Spanish policemen. "You blokes know how to use these?"

Both men nodded.

McCarter placed his AUG against the railing wall and readied his collection of minibombs.

Katz juggled the first of his grenades to get the heft of it. An accomplished thrower could get forty yards or more with one of the spheres. Tossing them in both directions over the promenade would provide almost enough cover. But it wouldn't keep the attackers from firing indiscriminately.

He waited grimly.

With a thunderous wailing of helicopter rotors, the nightmare swept in over the Ramblas.

AARON KURTZMAN CAUGHT the call from Kuwait City while Barbara Price was getting an interrogation room set up for their surprise guest. The Bear was a big, robust guy even sitting in the wheelchair behind his horseshoe-shaped desk in the computer room at Stony Man Farm.

World would have been more correctly the term used to describe the huge room. Besides his own command center, three other computer systems jibed into the matrix he was using to funnel information to and from the three different fronts of the Stony Man operation. The cybernetics center was dark, illuminated only by the various monitors the Intelligence team was using, and the three huge wall screens covered almost floor to ceiling in front and on both sides of him.

When the initiation point of the call logged in as Kuwait City on his computer screen via a cellular phone hookup through the United Nations camp, he knew of only one man who could have used the Farm's special number. He lifted the receiver and answered on the fourth ring. "Striker?"

"Hello, Aaron," the familiar voice said. "Your snitch turned up the goods, but I'm going to need some help getting to it."

"Name it."

"I need a schematic on the sewage system running from Jawhar Street to Salih Street."

"That's where the hostages are being kept?"

"That's what I've been told. It makes sense because those streets are among some of the worst-hit oil refinery areas of the Iraqi conflict. With the amount of rebuilding still going on in this city, it's possible that whole sections of the sewage system have been orphaned."

Kurtzman punched in computer commands, heard the hard disk boot in as electronic fingers diligently searched through the ready files he had on the Middle East and Kuwait City in particular.

The monitor flickered and changed. His fingers caressed the keys as he minimized the search sequence and brought the target area on-screen.

Across the room someone had opened up a window on one of the wall screens that broadcast a local news channel. Footage of Able Team's stand against the terrorists played across it. Whoever had opened the window on the screen froze the film time after time. The yellow circle materializing around different terrorists' heads let Kurtzman know the computer operator was reducing the pictures to computer-generated graphics. They'd be used for later comparison against Stony Man records or reproduced in Intel packages to be sent to the teams.

A street map appeared on the monitor, then melted away to leave the blueprints of the underlying sewage system. With the huge amounts of American labor presently being contracted for the rebuilding jobs in Kuwait, getting the files had been no trouble at all.

"Got 'em," Kurtzman said. "What do you need?"

"A description of what I can expect underground in the way of construction," Bolan replied.

Kurtzman complied, going back over the details as requested. Actual distances, twists, turns and the locations of a collection of manholes that would lead to the area in question—all contributed to the creation of a complete map Bolan needed.

"Anything else?" Kurtzman asked.

"Just stand by to push that special ID package through at the Kuwait end if necessary." Bolan then said goodbye and hung up.

Kurtzman heard the line go dead and automatically logged the time of the call so he could inform Barb when she came back on deck. Things were breaking so fast it was hard to keep an accurate time frame in mind.

He turned back to his present line of inquiries concerning the terrorist cells they knew about in the Middle East that had been connected to Saddam Hussein. He caught the emergency news broadcast about the bloody attack on the Olympic athletes in Barcelona out of the corner of his eye.

HAROUN KUBAISI LISTENED to the relayed communications from their American base intently as he steered his car through the confusing knot of Washington, D.C., midday traffic. At age twenty-eight, he'd only been driving for five years. Of that, he'd only spent six weeks in the United States. Four of those were during the present mission.

He kept both fists knotted around the wheel of the Ford Escort and wiped sweat from his face with the back of his hand. Rabi Adwan sat beside him, his long fingers wrapped around the muzzle of the Uzi machine pistol between his legs. Three more men sat in the back. Their weapons were laid loosely across the floorboards.

"Haroun," Abed Mansur's voice said urgently from the radio, "one of our brothers yet lives from the attack on the monument."

"Are you sure?" Kubaisi asked. He swept his dark gaze across the rearview mirror. A station wagon flying an inflatable pizza-delivery sign was honking behind him, riding his bumper as if trying to mate the two vehicles. The acne-faced young man behind the wheel drove seemingly without concern as his palm hit the dashboard in time with some enthusiastic rhythm.

"Yes. We were able to get a very clear picture of the scene. Timin was breathing when the rescue services picked him up and carried him away with the wounded Americans."

Kubaisi neatly cut off a pickup hauling a load of rolled sod and three shovels. With a blare of his horn, the pizza driver did the same.

"Where are they taking him?"

"From the street maps we have, and their present course, we believe they are taking him to Walter Reed Hospital."

"It's a military installation."

"Yes, but only loosely so. Security there is very thin. You'll have only a few problems getting inside."

"And once there?"

"Timin must be either freed or killed before he can give the Americans any information about us. Under their medications and truth serums, he may be fooled into divulging many of our secrets."

"I understand."

"Do not fail us, Haroun."

"No. God is with us on our mission. This is truly the coming of the great jihad. Our enemies will go broken and frightened before us. We'll drive them like cattle."

"Truly spoken, brother. May God keep you always in His sight."

"And you." Kubaisi broke the radio connection and hung up the microphone as Adwan traced a forefinger across the Washington, D.C. street map. He glanced in the rearview mirror at the three hard faces of the men sitting in the back seat.

Like him, they were committed to the actions they were asked to take now. They were *fedayeen*, men of sacrifice. If they died in this endeavor, their place in heaven with God was already assured.

"The hospital, brother?" he asked Adwan.

"I've found it."

"The directions, please."

He gave them.

As they pulled to a stop at the light on Seventeenth Street to make the turn onto Constitution Avenue, the pizza driver pulled up behind them. The driver honked, obviously wanting to turn right on the red light and frustrated at Kubaisi for signaling for a left turn.

Haroun Kubaisi's patience was gone. He'd been born a Palestinian peasant, had known the goodness of God in his heart since he was a small boy. Respect was a thing he'd given to others even while he was poor, even before he felt the calling to join the great jihad. And being something freely given, he expected it in return. Here in America, respect was a thing that had to be demanded.

He put the Escort into Park, then drew his 9 mm Taurus from under the seat. He'd decided that he'd rather pursue an ambulance than a pizza driver trying to beat a thirty-minute delivery deadline.

Getting out of the car, he ignored the increased frequency of the driver's honking. The lights changed to green, and the traffic began a slow surge forward. He kept the automatic tucked down beside his leg.

The driver saw him coming and quickly rolled up the window. A smug grin twisted the young man's face, and he gave Kubaisi the finger while he yelled insults that the Arab wouldn't have visited upon his worst enemy.

Kubaisi raised the pistol and fired three times through the window. The wagon sputtered and died shortly after the driver.

He felt better when he returned to the car and saw the light was still green. He put the Ford into gear and streaked off in pursuit of the ambulance carrying Timin to the hospital.

MACK BOLAN HOOKED his fingers into the manhole cover in the middle of the street and lifted. It didn't come easily. Made of iron, it weighed nearly a hundred pounds. The rumble of tank treads across street pavement less than a block away created vibrations that he could feel through his boot soles.

The warrior lowered himself through the opening, then pulled the cover back into place. The smell hit him at first. He took in a deep breath to immediately desensitize himself to the odor of rot and decay, then dipped a finger into the small jar of Mentholatum and applied the salve generously to his nostrils. When he took another breath, there was a definite decrease in odor.

Inky shadows covered the walls. According to Kurtzman's Intel, the walls were approximately fourteen feet apart. A four-foot shelf skirted either side of the stagnant sewer water. Something brittle popped under Bolan's shoe. He knelt briefly, touched the hard and jagged remains of a small animal's rib cage.

He straightened, dipped a hand into a pouch at his back and quickly affixed the silencer to the Walther MPK. It wouldn't help much. In the enclosed space of the sewage tunnel, the shots would seem loud anyway.

The warrior reached up, found the juncture between the brick ceiling and the concrete wall less than eighteen inches above him. He trailed his fingers along it to guide him in the darkness as he moved forward.

Bolan counted his steps. If Ghinzarli was right about where the terrorists were holding the American hostages, he'd entered the tunnel less than a quarter mile away. By his estimation, he'd covered most of that.

Pale yellow light gathered before him like early-morning mist. Fuzzy and gauzelike, it looked as substantial as a spiderweb. For a moment he had the impression that if he dragged a hand across it, he could tear it.

At the first sound of a rough voice speaking Arabic, the Executioner tightened his grip on the submachine gun and slowed his forward movement to a snail's pace. He had no idea how many men might be guarding the hostages. The tunnel twisted in a gradual forty-five-degree arc. He followed it, made himself as much a part of the wall as he could without touching it.

He waited just outside the fringe of weak illumination.

An emergency pump station opened out of a section of wall twenty feet ahead of him. Built without a door, one whole wall of the twenty-foot-by-thirty-foot room was revealed by the half-dozen oil lanterns hanging from the walls. Four guards dressed in robes with *ghutras* covering their heads maintained watch over the hostages.

Bolan counted at least three women in the ranks of the twenty-two prisoners. The Iraqi conflict had changed the face of war on several counts. From what the warrior could see of the military personnel, they hadn't been hurt yet.

The pump station was empty of equipment. The sewage control board had either reclaimed the pumps after the war the previous year, or the terrorists had cleared the room before the attack. The Americans stood or sat well away from the guards and the threat of the AK-47s they carried.

After a few minutes the guards shared a laugh, then one of them walked toward Bolan's position while slinging his assault rifle over his shoulder.

The Executioner put down the Walther and drew the Cold Steel Tanto knife from his boot. The edged metal whispered against leather. He waited on the guard, knew the man's night vision would be impaired by the vigil around the oil lanterns.

Bolan struck without warning, clapping a hand over the guard's lower face as the man drew abreast. The guard's hands were already fumbling with his robes to take care of nature's call. Before the man could do more than reach up and curl his fingers around Bolan's arm, the Executioner slipped the sharp blade between the guard's third and fourth ribs, slicing into the heart muscle neatly.

The guard convulsed and died a few seconds later.

Bolan wiped the bloody spittle from his hand and lowered the body gently to the concrete shelf. Now that the sewage channel proper was revealed in the lamplight, he saw that it was running slowly.

He frisked the corpse quickly, turned up a .38 revolver with a four-inch barrel and a few clips for the AK-47. He put those in a pile beside the assault rifle. Working carefully, he eased the dead man facedown into the brackish water. Once he was satisifed with the buoyancy, he pushed the corpse out and forward, letting the sluggish current take it back toward the guards.

He swept up the Walther in both hands, took his position against the wall and waited. The dead terrorist floated easily, almost in the center of the six-foot channel. The off-white robes stood out against the water, the material fanning out like a quarter moon.

With a cry of alarm, one of the guards drew the attention of the other two men and pointed at the floating body slowly approaching them. The man who'd yelled put his weapon to one side and ran to the edge of the concrete shelf. On his knees, he flailed for the corpse. Water splashed over him, and his fingertips just brushed against the robes.

Satisfied the American prisoners weren't in any way in his direct line of fire, the Executioner squeezed the Walther's trigger. A line of 9 mm parabellums slammed into the two terrorists standing at the edge of the channel peering down at their companion's efforts to save the dead man. Their bodies twisted and pirouetted. Then, released from the impact of the bullets, the two corpses joined the third in the water.

The fourth man dived into the water.

Bolan threw himself into motion. He dropped the empty submachine gun as he skidded into place between the surviving terrorist and the American soldiers. Their shouts of concern and surprise filled his ears, made it impossible to hear any movement the terrorist might make. He reached over his shoulder and unslung the Mossberg Bullpup 12.

The terrorist surfaced ten feet farther down the channel and came up with both hands wrapped around a Soviet Tokarev. Twin muzzle-flashes sprouted from the pistol a heartbeat apart as the Arab screamed in rage and fear.

One round whistled by Bolan's face; the other smashed into his Kevlar vest.

The Executioner fired two Magnum double-ought rounds from the Mossberg. The first pattern hit the terrorist in the chest and forced his body up against the resistant surge of water. The second blew his head apart like a rotten grapefruit. Mercifully the decapitated corpse slid under the water in seconds.

Several of the hostages were on their feet when Bolan turned to face them. For the first time he saw the chains threaded through the manacles on their wrists that connected them to eyebolts drilled into the floor.

"It's okay," he said in a reassuring voice. "I'm with the American military. I'm here to get you out." He passed a multipurpose tool to a young Marine sergeant.

A ragged cheer ran through the hostages. A second lieutenant in a torn Army dress uniform started assuming command over the group and ordered them to silence.

Bolan took up a point position and recovered his Walther submachine gun as he stood guard.

The snick of the wire cutters chewing through the chain was audible and echoed across the tunnel.

The lieutenant took two men with him to the concrete shelf overlooking the dark water. A corporal waded in and recovered the bodies. They stripped the corpses of weapons while the sergeant finished releasing the rest of the prisoners. The officer took an AK-47 and shoved a handful of clips into his trouser pockets. He gave orders to his people, got them formed quickly into a single line, then joined Bolan. He thrust out a hand. "I'm Second Lieutenant Bart Jamison," he said in a clear voice. "I can take over from here."

Bolan took the hand briefly. "I'm Colonel Rance Pollock, and I appreciate your offering your services, but I'm quite capable."

The lieutenant snapped back his hand after it was released, squared his shoulders and fired off a fast salute. "Yes, sir. No disrespect intended, sir."

"None taken, Lieutenant. How many men were guarding you people?"

"Six."

"Where are the other two?"

"I have no idea, sir. They left—" he flicked a glance at his wristwatch "—approximately twenty-five minutes ago."

"None of your people speak Arabic?"

"No, sir. I asked when we were first thrown together. Our Intel regarding their probable actions is severely limited."

"Then getting out of here as quietly and as quickly as possible would seem to be our best bet."

"Yes, sir."

"See to it. I'll bring up the rear with one other man."

"Yes, sir." The lieutenant turned and gave out orders. A Marine gunney carrying one of the recovered assault rifles headed up the group and got them started out.

Bolan got the gunney's attention, then tossed the Marine a flashlight from his pack. "If you encounter resistance, it goes out."

The gunney nodded and saluted.

"If you don't mind my saying so," the lieutenant said, "it's unusual to find a colonel out in the field."

"These are unusual times," Bolan replied with more than a hint of authority to quell the man's suspicions. The Pollock name carried weight behind it in the form of a thick eyes-only document bearing the presidential seal. If the lieutenant tried checking on the name when he returned to base, there was enough documentation to prove there *was* a Colonel Rance Pollock who'd been called in from retirement. And there was also enough flak to keep the guy from inquiring any further. "Get up there and get your people out of here, Lieutenant."

"Yes, sir."

Bolan motioned to the young sergeant who'd unshackled his fellow Americans. "Your name?"

"Sergeant Anthony McSwain, Colonel." He saluted and returned the multipurpose tool.

Bolan unslung the Walther. "Do you know how to use one of these, Sergeant?"

"Yes, sir. With a certain fondness, I might add."

Bolan passed over the submachine gun, adding four extra clips. "When the time is right, then, and only on my signal."

"Yes, sir."

The last of the ex-hostages disappeared from immediate sight. The flashlight was a bouncing will-o'-the-wisp far down the tunnel.

Savage yells erupted from the other end of the tunnel, echoing for a moment in the empty pump station. The sound of running feet reverberated between the concrete walls, followed almost instantly by the appearance of hand torches coming around a bend in the shaft.

"Looks like you got us out just before they transported us, sir." The sergeant clutched the Walther MPK grimly, held it waist high as he set himself. "We're standing between them and a lot of unarmed soldiers."

"Yeah," Bolan replied as he looked around, "but this is no place for a last stand."

From the looks of the approaching crowd, there were at least a dozen men running toward them. If they stayed pat, they'd give their lives to gain only moments for the fleeing group. And that wouldn't be enough.

"Sergeant," the Executioner called.

"Yes, sir."

"The lanterns."

"Yes, sir."

Bolan slung the combat shotgun over his shoulder, then blew out the oil lamps and tore them from the walls. He carried three of them to the edge of the concrete shelf as a few stray shots started to blister the walls around them.

"Down." Bolan yanked on the man's arm. "Crack the oil reservoirs open and drain them over the water." Bolan demonstrated, stiking the first lantern on the concrete edge between his hands like an egg and draining the thick fluid out. Within seconds all six had been emptied, then dropped into the water.

The terrorists were fifty yards away and closing. Their flashlights threw bouncing shadows over the ceiling and walls, the bullets coming faster now.

McSwain gave out a cry of pain then toppled over, grabbing at his shoulder.

On the move already, Bolan reached out and helped the young sergeant to his feet and got him headed down the tunnel. Two rounds hammered into the Kevlar vest over the Executioner's kidneys. Once the sergeant had settled into a stumbling run, the warrior reached into his webbing and selected an incendiary grenade and an M45C Comboball.

He halted, spun, pulled the pin on the incendiary first and lobbed it in a sidearm throw into the water where the terrorists' lights reflected with an oily darkness.

McSwain dropped into a kneeling crouch a short distance behind him and opened up with the Walther. Nine mm bullets skipped and spun from the walls. The terrorist advance was brought to a brief stop, and their firing became erratic.

Bolan counted two full seconds, then pulled the pin on the Comboball and threw it like a Nolan Ryan fastball into the center of the terrorists. It went off a second and a half later. A white cloud of CS gas spread around the terrorists quickly as they dived for cover and cried out in pain from the marble-sized soft-rubber balls smacking into their flesh. Before they could recover, the incendiary in the water went off.

The volatile mixture of Thermite TH3 and First Fire Mixture VII wouldn't be denied by the water surrounding it. Waves splashed against the walls and ceiling. Flames shot up like a fiery typhoon, and the lamp oil spread out over the surface of the water ignited instantly. Patches of fire flew out over the walls, ceiling and terrorists, clinging to whatever they hit. In seconds several of the terrorists were on fire. A line of flames danced in the channel almost twenty feet long.

McSwain had reloaded and was working 3- and 5-round bursts from the submachine gun. "Go ahead, sir," the sergeant said as he dumped the second magazine and fitted a third into place. "I'll hold them off as long as I can."

Bolan looped a hand under the man's arm and lifted. "On your feet, Sergeant. That's an order. I didn't come this far to leave anybody behind."

3

Hal Brognola approached Stony Man Farm by helicopter. His mind was already churning with the possibilities of what might lie before himself and his teams. The United States had only finished one war little more than a year ago. He didn't think the American people were ready for another one, especially one that promised to strike so quickly and so deadly on home soil.

The view from the sky was breathtaking. The hardsite that was nestled in the Blue Ridge Mountains of Virginia took its name directly from Stony Man Mountain. From the air the "stone face" along the profile of the mountain couldn't really be seen for what it was. But Brognola knew where it was, and his eyes were drawn to it just the same. It never failed to give him a firmer resolve no matter what kind of odds lay before him.

To the west was Shenandoah Valley where General Stonewall Jackson marched his troops at a pace that showed the achievements possible when the human spirit fired the body. To the consternation of the North, Jackson's troops had appeared to be everywhere, had given the impression that they were five and six times their actual numbers. They were successful in their efforts, and bought time for the rest of the Confederate armies to gather.

On a lot of days Brognola knew just how that long-ago warhorse must have felt. Like Jackson, the head Fed often found himself asking the impossible of his people. Phoenix Force and Able Team had to be everywhere at once within their own respective spheres of influence. There was no one else to do the jobs they were asked to do. By the time covert action reached the truly legitimate agencies of the United States government, things were often just one heartbeat this side of Hell. And they had no choice but to fight like five or six men each to meet the challenges that came their way.

Although he was no longer officially part of the Stony Man operation by his own decision, Mack Bolan was still the spearhead for the group. The Executioner had been flinging fire back in the face of the savages and cannibals somewhere along the front line since before the inception of Stony Man Farm. It had been Bolan's dream in a sense, built partly to his specs and designed for quick-strike missions. But the big warrior had found the dream too limiting for the forces that drove him. In the end Bolan had had no choice but to go back out into the world and challenge the predators where he found them. For him the protective walls of Stony Man Farm had also proved to be too insulating. By the time they became aware of a threat, Bolan figured he was already a half-step off the lead.

Brognola took an antacid tablet from his jacket, chewed it and swallowed it. He knew the men who made up the striking fists of Stony Man Farm hadn't joined for the pay or the glory, but that didn't stop him from wishing they got a little more recognition out of their efforts occasionally.

The helicopter pilot called for clearance to land and was quickly given an affirmative.

They lost altitude as the descent began, and the Farm itself came into view. The main building was an L-shaped three-story affair. Two outbuildings and a tractor barn were east, west and south of the main house.

Apple and peach orchards stood in neat rows along the outskirts of the productive regions of the Farm. The inner fields grew sweet potatoes, strawberries and snap beans. Three farmhands tilled the grounds with John Deere tractors as the helicopter passed over. Two pickups rattled along carrying seed and farm implements in their beds. The field hands were denim-clad cowboys who worked the land and dug postholes with the best of them. But their learning didn't end there. They also knew all about the Uzis and automatic pistols they were required to carry and wear during their shifts.

An assortment of equipment was hidden in the surrounding grounds. Surveillance cameras and electrified fences were camouflaged by the forest, along with the armed guards and dogs who patrolled them. Closer to the house, more cameras and motion detectors overlapped each other, making penetration almost impossible.

Brognola wouldn't say anything was impossible concerning Farm security since the attack years ago that had taken such a heavy toll, but since the reconstruction, the defensive measures were as close to perfection as they could get. The perimeters hadn't been penetrated since. They'd been attacked once, but they'd held their own.

The helicopter touched down at the small landing strip north of the main house. Brognola got out, and the pilot took off again immediately. The wind whipped up dust all around the Fed as he hunkered down and ran toward the waiting jeep. When the dust cleared and he blinked his eyes free of debris, he saw Leo Turrin lounging behind the wheel.

"Gee," Brognola growled as he stepped up into the passenger seat, "they're letting just about anybody into this little shindig."

"You know," Turrin said as he hit the starter and turned the vehicle back around to the narrow road leading to the main house, "when I saw you, I thought the same thing."

Brognola stuck out his hand, and Turrin took it. "Glad to see you, Leo."

The stocky little Fed nodded. He looked as rumpled as ever, and his mustache needed a trim. "Wish it could have been under more pleasant circumstances."

Leo Turrin was still the man's name in some circles. But those circles were Mafia, and he'd unofficially retired after Bolan's war against the capos. Most days now he wore a new name: Leonard Justice. He worked out of the Justice Department now instead of being an undercover agent working organized crime as a born-into-the-blood member of the Black Hand. Of all the Stony Man people, he'd known Bolan the longest. His cover had been so good back in those days that the Executioner had nearly left one of his trademark marksman's medals on Turrin's corpse.

"Any word?"

"Able's at Walter Reed. The docs are working on the terrorist, but it looks like touch and go for now. Phoenix is engaged heavily with a four-helicopter hit squad from a Jordanian freighter. There have already been some casualties there, too."

Brognola took another antacid tablet. "And Striker?"

"No word. Grimaldi's in touch with the Bear now from Kuwait City. As soon as Jack knows something, he'll be on the horn to us."

"What about the visitor you brought us?"

Turrin grinned with true humor. "Wael Boudia is definitely not a happy camper. He hasn't been since two federal marshals took him out of protective custody early this morning. He keeps yammering about the rights granted to him by the U.S. Constitution."

One of Turrin's jobs was to help oversee the Witness Protection Program. With his unofficial mob connections, he was often able to tip the OrgCrime people with names of individuals who were ready to play ball with the Justice Department. It was there they'd found access to Boudia, who'd defected to the West during the Iraq conflict shortly before war had broken out.

"So what are you telling him?" Brognola asked.

"I told him to dream on."

"Where is he?"

"At the Farm. We rigged up an interrogation room. Aaron's fixing up a picture show for you and Barb to use when you interview him."

"Does he know why he was brought here?"

"It hasn't been mentioned yet. But Boudia's a smart guy. When the news about the attack on Kuwait City broke this morning, our boy was already packing a bag by the time the marshals got there to put the arm on him. Somewhere along the way, without the program people knowing it, Boudia had put together a nest egg of a quarter-million dollars. Interesting, no?"

"Hell, yes," Brognola said as the Farm's main house came into view.

GARY MANNING WRESTLED the three-foot section of pipe through the fire escape door of the building, then lugged it out onto the roof. Made of steel, with a four-inch plug welded into place and packed with his own brand of special ingredients, it weighed over sixty pounds. He was perspiring heavily, and his breathing was ragged when he reached the low parapet overlooking the street. He set the pipe down and unslung his gear.

Two of the helicopters were in sight now. From their position, he guessed they were approaching in standard two-by-two diamond formation. The signature was military, but he knew the Jordanian freighter captain would still deny involvement.

Pandemonium reigned in the promenade below. Twilight allowed most of the details to be seen, but white smoke billowed up from the grenades McCarter and Katz had spread across the street.

To the right of him, he heard the flat, echoing cracks of Calvin James's Beretta sniper rifle banging away. The roar of the helicopters' rotors sounded like the thunder and crack of giant vultures' wings as they descended. That noise faded into the background when the .50-caliber machine guns erupted from under the bellies of the aircraft.

The bullets raked like sharp talons across the buildings, slicing through the smoky membrane stretched across the promenade. Glass exploded from windows; potted plants danced off white-painted, wrought-iron balconies, screams littered the open space between the lines of buildings. Not everyone had had time to get clear.

Manning lifted the pipe and settled it onto his shoulder. He'd made the pleasant discovery of a machine shop in one of the ground-floor offices, which was designed to produce metal artwork. Lengths of pipe, angle iron and different kinds of wire of various gauges had been stored haphazardly against three of the walls. The cutting and welding torches had been top-notch.

Once he'd seen the four-inch pipe and barrel containing a loose collection of metal bits that had been torched off of past sculptures, an idea had taken root in Manning's mind.

Despite their permission to be in-country to protect the American Olympic athletes, the Spanish government hadn't given permission for the team to carry heavy armament.

Manning figured the thirty-seven minutes he'd spent down in the machine shop had made up for some of that oversight. With the plug in place as best as he could weld it, he'd stuffed in the pipe gunpowder from an assortment of grenades and dynamite that were in the personal pack he always carried. He'd added a length of fuse from his explosives gear and left it hanging out the hole he'd drilled near the plugged end of the pipe. Then he'd shoveled in fistfuls of chopped metal, angle iron and curved crescents of cut pipe no bigger than a silver dollar.

The end result was a portable cannon in the broadest sense of both words.

The helicopters banked for a second run. All four of them were visible now. The smoke was clearing off the promenade, and Manning could see bodies scattered on the street.

With no true aiming mechanism, the Phoenix fighter had to rely on line of sight. He took his lighter from his pocket as he zeroed in on the lead attack chopper. The flame touched the fuse and ignited it. The pipe cannon went off without warning, the recoil knocking the big Canadian on his ass.

He looked up, flat on his back, and saw the helicopter he'd aimed at wobble as thick, black smoke belched from it. Huge holes had been torn into its Plexiglas bubble and its fuselage by the flying shrapnel. Abruptly it heeled over, out of control.

The main rotor chopped into a rooftop, and the rest of the helicopter followed it down. As the chopper touched down on its side, it was consumed by a thunderous explosion. Nothing survived the rolling blast of flame that followed.

Still dazed from the force the cannon had expended in the opposite direction, Manning pushed himself to his feet and looked for the pipe. "Son of a bitch," he said when he saw the pipe appeared to still be intact. Heated metal glowed red at its mouth. He pulled on his gloves.

The three helicopters swarmed in confusion overhead for just a moment, then began another attack run. Machine-gun fire rattled into the promenade, rockets sizzling after them.

After checking to make sure no burning embers remained inside the pipe, Manning took a pouch of measured powder from his belt, sliced the end of it open with his Gerber knife and let it leak down to the bottom of the pipe. He poured in a sackful of metal shrapnel after it. A length of fuse, already cut, was poked into the fuse hole with a mechanical pencil.

One of the helicopter pilots had spotted him and flew toward him. The belly-mounted machine gun blazed ceaselessly. Fifty-caliber slugs ripped corners from the brickwork as Manning lined up his make-shift weapon. A rocket slammed into the building's top story, the roof rocking in response. The Phoenix warrior absorbed the shock with his legs, straightened the cannon's wobble, then touched the fuse with his reclaimed lighter.

The cannon fired and exploded.

Manning was blown back by the concussion. He had a brief impression of the helicopter coming apart less than thirty feet above him, flaming wreckage spinning through the air like comets. Then his head hit one of the exhaust fans mounted on the roof and he blacked out.

CALVIN JAMES HIT the transmit button on his throat-ear headset as the two remaining helicopters broke off their attack run. "Manning. Manning, come in."

Silence.

"Has anybody seen Manning?" he radioed.

"Looked like that bloody helicopter came down right on top of him, mate," McCarter answered.

James thought it looked that way, too.

Katz's voice was calm when he broke into the conversation, but James could sense the emotion behind their leader's clipped words. Phoenix Force had already lost one of their own. James's membership was proof of that. He hadn't been one of the original members. He'd been pulled in to replace Keio Ohara.

"Focus on those remaining helicopters," Katz said. "If there's anything we can do for Gary later, we will. At this moment our responsibility is to those people down there."

James didn't like it, but he had to agree. They took their lives in their hands every time they went out on a mission. And the objective was always the same: the prevention of loss of lives by others.

He fitted his eye to the scope and let out his breath as the cross hairs centered over the pilot's side of the Plexiglas bubble. Jagged holes in the plastic were silent testimony to the skill he'd already employed. He just hadn't been able to hit the pilot.

The helicopter's course across the sky was erratic. It bounced and skipped as it tracked back on-line with the promenade. It had exhausted the rocket pods and the chain gun, but the two passengers still wreaked havoc with a pair of AK-47/M-203 combinations. The 40 mm grenade launchers scored impartial hits against everything below. A car flipped over in the wake of the latest pass. Another grenade landed in a flower stall and blew away pots, blossoms and the two people who'd been taking cover behind it.

On the pilot now as the chopper came around in profile, James squeezed through the remaining fourteen rounds in the clip. The 7.62 mm rounds chipped through the Plexiglas, tore padding from the pilot's chair and punched holes into the instrument panel.

Black smoke roiled from the instrument panel, filling the Plexiglas bubble in a matter of seconds.

James figured it for an electrical fire as he fed a fresh magazine into the M-21. If it was, the acrid smoke had to be burning the eyes of the men inside.

When the side panel of the helicopter was pushed open to let the smoke out James swept in with the scope. The cross hairs locked on the pilot's head, and he squeezed the trigger.

The pilot's head jerked, then his body slumped over the yoke. The helicopter slid out of control, arcing out over Barcelona's dock area. Less than a moment later it slammed into a freighter just above the waterline.

The way the chopper came apart and slid down the steel side reminded James of a bug hitting a windshield. "*Sayonara,* sucker," he said grimly. Then he turned to search for the last helicopter.

If Gary Manning had bought it, the black Phoenix Force member meant to see that his friend didn't go down unavenged.

THE HOSPITAL REMINDED Carl Lyons of all the other times he'd stood the deathwatch. He paced restlessly before the double doors, aware of the eyes from the nurses' station watching him.

He didn't care. A lot of years had passed since he'd stopped caring.

Pacing was something he did at hospitals. Often it had helped keep his mind off whether a fellow policeman in an operating room was dying.

Mixed in there, too, were a number of blurred memories of personal trips to hospitals for wounds received in various sorties.

Schwarz and Blancanales sat in the waiting room flipping through magazines and exchanging small talk with two uniforms and a plainclothesman who'd accompanied them to the hospital.

He envied them their peace of mind. His own was crowded with images of the bloody aftermath in the park. Occasionally the nurses' eyes would switch from his pacing to the Colt Python rigged upside down under his arm.

He paused and gazed through the wire-meshed windows, willed the operating room's door to open and end the uncertainty.

"Don't stop now, Ironman," Blancanales called out from behind him.

Lyons scowled at the man's shadowy image in the glass.

"Yeah," Schwarz chimed in. "Me and Pol got a bet going. He says the floor's going to give out first. I say you'll wear the soles off those boots before that happens."

"Hey," one of the uniforms said as he leaned forward, "who's betting on the floor? I want a piece of that action."

Lyons gave them the bird without turning around.

In the glass the reflections of the three women standing at the nurses' station turned quickly away to hide smiles of amusement.

The uniformed policemen and the plainclothesman weren't going to be privy to the interrogation Able Team had in store for the terrorist, provided the man survived. They were there solely in a backup capacity. Their captain hadn't been happy about the situation, but the Justice Department liaison hadn't offered a choice.

A man with dark, swarthy features wearing doctor's blues walked into the corridor. He tied a mask over his lower face.

Other people had passed through the corridor on their way to the different operating rooms, but none had set off Lyons's cop-trained trouble radar.

This one filled his head with a jangle like a cymbal-clapping windup monkey gone mad.

Lyons rested a big hand against the door and leaned in closer. The doctor's blouse wasn't cut for the pistol stuck in the waistband.

"Hey, buddy," Lyons said as he pushed through the door. He flicked the restraint strap from the Python, palmed the weapon and brought it into view. He was aware of Blancanales and Schwarz going into motion behind him, trailed by the Washington, D.C., crew.

The dark man spun, his hand dropping inside the blouse and coming out with a stubby automatic pistol.

Lyons shot him through the face mask just below the nose.

The terrorist went flying backward and slumped against the wall. Down the corridor a nurse dropped a tray of medical instruments that clattered across the floor just ahead of her scream.

"Down, Carl!" Schwarz ordered.

Lyons dived at once, spread over the breadth of the polished floor as a swarm of bullets tore through the air where he'd been standing.

Schwarz's Beretta fired twice. Return fire was immediate.

Lyons tracked the hostile bullets, saw three men run into the corridor through the fire-escape door. He tightened his grip on the .357 and raised it into target acquisition.

DAVID MCCARTER ABANDONED the Steyr AUG when it clicked dry. He knew he'd hit the approaching helicopter because he could see the ragged line of bullet holes across the bubble nose.

With a smooth economy of motion, he drew the Browning Hi-Power from shoulder leather and leveled it before him. In Her Majesty's Special Air Service he'd been taught to shoot without aiming. It was a form of pistolwork designed especially for the counterterrorist measures he'd been involved in.

He employed the same method now, as the helicopter flew almost level with him. Instead of targeting the men aboard the craft, he shot for the rear rotor. Sparks flashed as his bullets scored. He ran the magazine dry, only then hearing the ragged chatter coming from the tail section.

Abruptly the helicopter went spinning out of control. One of the gunners was flung off, the terrorist screaming to his death, arms and legs flailing as if he were trying to find running room in the air.

The tail of the helicopter struck a building past the promenade proper and snapped off. The whirling-dervish effect caused by the ruined rear rotor stopped at once when the Plexiglas bubble smashed into another building on the other side of the street. The main rotor shattered and threw steel shrapnel in all directions. Then the aircraft dropped like a stone and crushed a Volkswagen microbus parked below. Figures inside the wrecked helicopter moved when it came to a rest.

When he looked over his shoulder after retrieving the AUG, McCarter found that Katz and the two Spaniards were already moving. He had to work to catch up. He jumped over the roof railing and bruised his hip against the side of the fire escape as he made the corner. He had both weapons reloaded before he reached the third-floor landing.

"Rafael," Katz barked into the headset.

"Yes, Yakov."

"The last helicopter is down, but some of its occupants are still alive."

"I'm moving on it now."

So was McCarter. And he had every intention of not being the last man to arrive.

THE SOUND OF GUNFIRE revived Gilead Nidal. His mouth felt as if it was stuffed with cotton, and his throat hurt. One look at his surroundings told the man he was in a hospital operating room.

His eyes were bleary, refusing to focus long on one object. He tried to swallow but couldn't.

More gunfire sounded.

He focused on it, used it to fuel synapses that refused to come under his will. With an effort he sat up on the operating table. He could see better once the bright lights were out of his face.

He took a ragged breath, then another. His head felt clearer with each one.

Then he noticed the operating team gathered around the door. They stared through the inset window in obvious disbelief.

Nidal was certain another cell of the jihad forces was trying to effect his rescue. Or, if they couldn't, to ensure his death. He felt no fear. For the first time in his twenty years, he felt totally committed to something. For the first time since the American bombing of Baghdad, he felt truly safe.

God had laid his hands upon Nidal's soul. He'd been charged with a sacred duty that he couldn't fail to discharge.

With an effort he took a stumbling step away from the operating table. A bruised, blackened area over the right side of his chest had a row of bloody stitches holding an incision together. Tubes ran from the back of one of his hands and the inside of his other arm to bags hanging from the hooks of gleaming skeletal structures.

He knotted the plastic lines in his fist and jerked. The IV needles tore through his flesh, and a scream died unborn in his tortured throat. He closed his fingers over one of the bloody, razor-sharp scalpels lying on the instrument tray. The metal structures holding the bag of blood and whatever medicines they'd been giving him crashed to the floor. Dark and clear liquids raced across the waxed surface.

The group at the window turned to face him.

Nidal guessed there were seven of them. His vision blurred to the point that he truly didn't know. He felt the warmth of blood spill down his stomach and legs from the rips in his arm and hand, and from the incision on his chest.

"Put down that knife, you son of a bitch," A big man growled.

Nidal didn't respond. There was no need, even if he was able.

The man lunged unexpectedly.

Instinctively Nidal's knife hand licked out, flashed as it passed across both of the man's outstretched hands. The cuts across the man's palms went to the bone and sprayed blood instantly.

The man went stumbling back, his breath coming in hoarse gasps of pain. The other members of the operating-room staff closed in to help their fellow.

Nidal knew he couldn't fight them all. He didn't even believe he could stay conscious much longer. His senses swam dizzyingly.

With a prayer on his lips, he lifted the knife again.

RAFAEL ENCIZO KNEW all about the value of the element of surprise when launching attacks. As a one-time member of a CIA-sponsored anti-Castro force in his native Cuba, he was accustomed to using surprise as a weapon, and having it used against him. But he was damned if he knew who was more surprised by the present turn of events when the terrorist helicopter plunged out of the sky and squashed the VW microbus.

He'd been covering the ground floor of the operation, tied in to radio communications with the Spanish police force because he could speak the language better than McCarter and James. Katz and Manning couldn't speak it at all. Until the helicopter dropped, he'd been helping in sorting out the injured and the dead from the scores of bodies littering the promenade. The cries of the wounded and dying still rang in his ears when he charged the terrorist aircraft.

Flames curled up from the tail rotor and quickly spread to the nose bubble. As two shadows drifted away from the rubble, a muzzle-flash spit death from the wall of the building.

Encizo ducked quickly and leveled his Uzi at the shadow's midsection. He stroked the trigger, coaxed out a 3-round burst that dumped the shadow onto the sidewalk.

A muffled explosion sounded from the bowels of the helicopter, which jumped in a death spasm that looked like the last reflexive kick of a crushed grasshopper. More fire raced along the metal sides of the chopper and threw fresh light into the immediate area.

The fiery glare was both help and hindrance. For a moment Encizo had lost the remaining man. Then the terrorist stood up from the broken hull with his assault rifle clutched at waist level in both hands.

Ecizo threw himself to one side just ahead of the bullets that scarred the pavement where he'd been standing. He rolled twice, listened to the sweep of the AK-47 as it closed in on him, then heard the bolt click empty. The wiry Cuban pushed himself up on one hand, held the Uzi in the other and moved in at a dead run. He wanted to take the man alive if he could. But he wasn't given the opportunity.

The terrorist lifted a pistol and aimed it point-blank at the Phoenix Force warrior.

Encizo dropped and slid forward on his stomach, his shirt ripped to shreds. The Kevlar vest beneath protected the flesh beneath from the same fate, but his elbow was scraped severely as he pulled the Uzi into target acquisition. The burst caught the terrorist across the face and stutter-stepped the corpse back into the flames clinging to the helicopter.

Warm blood trickling down his arm from the torn elbow, Encizo got to his feet and looked at the helicopter. Nothing else moved.

"Rafael?" Katz asked.

"I'm okay," he said, then realized the Phoenix Force leader was standing beside him and released the transmit button on the throat-ear headset.

"I thought the bugger had you there for a moment, mate," McCarter said.

"Me too," Encizo replied truthfully.

"I've got Manning," James said over the radio.

Encizo reloaded his weapon and peered up at the building where the burly Canadian had been stationed. A small knot of tension unfurled in his stomach when he saw James standing with Manning's arm stretched across his shoulders.

"Where'd he get the cannon?" McCarter asked.

Slinging the Uzi, Encizo followed Katz out onto the field of the dead. Other people joined them when they realized the danger had passed. A moment of panic drove the bystanders back to cover as a pair of helicopters hovered into view above the Ramblas.

"Made it myself," Manning said in a groggy voice.

"I've seen pipe bombs that were put together better," James said. "This sucker's peeled back like a banana. It's a damn miracle it didn't take his head off when he touched it off."

"Need any help with him?" McCarter asked.

"No. We'll see you at the bottom shortly."

Encizo heard McCarter swear as the Briton trailed close behind. During his days as a revolutionary, Encizo had seen a number of atrocities. He'd never foolishly believed he could become used to them. A warrior never got used to death. If he did, he was no longer even truly human. And the trip back to humanity was a lot farther than the trip away.

Most of the victims were half his age. Their hopes and dreams had been snuffed without ever knowing the light of day. It hurt to look at them. He kept his emotions locked in. He knew the others would do the same. There would be time for mourning later.

CARL LYONS WINCED as a stray round from a terrorist's pistol burned across the back of his calf. He moved the Python's sights over the middle Arab's chest and dropped the hammer. The .357 Magnum round slammed the guy back into the fire-escape door, the body sliding across the release bar and opening the door a few inches. Neither of the remaining terrorists tried to escape.

A body came stumbling forward and interfered with Lyons's aim. One of the uniformed cops hit the floor with his face, and stayed there. Blood pooled from the huge wound in the back of his head.

Recognizing that Able Team had become trapped in a deadly cross fire, Lyons rolled to his feet facing in the other direction.

A fourth terrorist stood in the hallway behind the white-suited nurse who'd dropped the medical tray.

The man had his free arm up under the woman's jaw, held her locked tightly to him. The muzzle of the nickel-plated automatic was screwed tightly to the nurse's temple. The skin beneath the barrel was white from the pressure.

"Halt, American!" the terrorist ordered. "Halt now, or I will shoot this woman's head from her very shoulders!"

Lyons kept his weapon aimed at the two bodies in an instinctive Weaver's stance. Only the hint of a shadow seemed to separate them. "Pol. Gadgets." He was dimly aware that the gunfire behind him had ceased. It didn't keep his shoulder blades from tightening in expectation of a bullet in his back. His thumb rolled back the hammer of the Python.

"I see him," Blancanales said.

"It's your call, Ironman," Schwarz added.

The nurse struggled and tried to scream. The terrorist yanked her back into place and popped the underside of her chin forcibly with the forearm used to restrain her. Her scream mutated into a low cry of muffled pain.

"The other two?" Lyons asked. He returned the baleful gaze of the terrorist full measure.

"Down and out," Blancanales reported.

Static from the police walkie-talkies hanging from the uniforms' belts vibrated through the air.

"Put your weapons down," the terrorist commanded.

"Can't do it," Lyons replied in a calm voice.

"Then the woman will die."

Frightened tears ran down the woman's face. She obviously wasn't standing on her own anymore.

Shouting voices came from inside the operating room.

Focused on his target, Lyons didn't take the time to look. "Pol, you got the door? There might be more of them inside."

"I got it, guy."

"The woman will die if you don't put your weapons down," the terrorist repeated. "Her blood will be on your hands. I come here bathed in the glory of God, sent to do His mission against the American Satans. Whether I live or die, it doesn't matter. I'll go to live with Him when I leave this mortal vale."

The operating room door burst open, and shocked voices echoed in the hall.

Instinctively the terrorist turned to face the new threat.

Lyons fired. His bullet cored into the terrorist's exposed gun arm, shattered the forearm before passing through. The pistol came away from the nurse's head, then fired into the wall. Lyons fired again, as coolly as if he were on a target range back in the academy. The second bullet took the terrorist in the heart, followed immediately by a third. The final round snapped the terrorist's head back and toppled him through the second-story window behind him.

The corpse disappeared in a shower of broken glass.

"It's checkout time for this mortal vale, pal," Lyons said in a harsh whisper. He flicked open the Python's cylinder and shook out the brass. A brief twist of a speedloader and he was fully chambered again.

Blancanales caught the nurse as she started to drop to her knees. The plainclothes detective called out orders into his walkie-talkie and ordered approaching units to seal off the hospital. The uniformed policeman dropped down to check on his partner, but Lyons already knew there was nothing to be done.

A doctor, his mask hanging down around his neck, stood in the corridor in front of the operating room. He was pale-faced and breathing rapidly. He pointed back into the O.R. "Christ! There's a crazy man in there! He—" His voice choked to a stop as he saw the carnage in the hallway. "What the hell's going on out here?"

Lyons and Schwarz blitzed by the doctor, pushing him down and away out of possible line of fire. A flood of O.R. personnel swarmed into the hall. Lyons lifted the Magnum, and the flood parted.

Beyond them the surgery was in disarray. The terrorist they'd loaded into the ambulance from the war monument attack lay in a twisted knot on the floor by the operating table. Bloody IV lines were snarled underneath him. A sharp edge in his hand glinted from the pod of powerful lights overhead. The ruler-straight edges of his cut throat gaped obscenely.

Lyons had to admire the man's guts. The slash across his throat was nearly from ear to ear and almost textbook perfect.

"He killed himself," the doctor said at Lyons's side. "He took the knife when no one was watching. Then he...he...killed himself."

"Did a damn fine job of it, too," Lyons replied. He leathered the .357, turned and started to go past the doctor.

The doctor grabbed his arm. "What kind of people are these?"

"Believers," Lyons answered. "And that's the worst kind of enemy you can have."

4

Not much remained of the face depicted on the computer monitor. At least two bullets had torn through the left cheekbone and right eye. Blue-black bruises from the impacts mottled the pallid skin. Most of the upper right ear was missing. Evidently the bullet that penetrated the eye had gone in at an angle, bounced, then broken free through the lesser resistance offered by the soft tissue in the auditory canal. There was no blood other than that within the wounds themselves. The corpse had been washed up before having its picture taken.

Aaron Kurtzman rolled his wheelchair to a stop beside Huntington Wethers's workstation, propped his elbows on the arms and watched with avid interest. "How's it coming?"

Wethers nodded as his hands tapped the white keyboard in syncopation. He shifted his empty pipe to the side of his mouth. "Good. Real good. This is going to be the tenth one that we wouldn't have had a chance of identifying without the program. Still got a stack of them to go, though."

"How're you holding up?"

"I'm in for the duration," Wethers replied.

"If there's anything I can do, let me know."

Wethers murmured an affirmative, then leaned back in his chair to let the computer program take over.

Even though he'd had a hand in designing the software they were using for identifying the terrorists, Kurtzman still found himself mystified when he saw it in operation. It was a variation based in part on the program Barrows and Sadler had written for the National Center for Missing and Exploited Children.

The monitor flickered as the cursor passed back and forth across the screen. It dropped in pieces of pigment as it worked, took longer when it got to sections where more of the face was missing or showed trauma. Gradually, like a magnetic jigsaw puzzle pulling pieces into itself, the picture became complete.

Once the program was finished, nothing remained of the gunshot wounds. A whole face looked back at them. Except Kurtzman could still see death in the dark eyes. It was present even in the computer-generated face. Maybe someone less schooled in the difference might not notice, but he did.

"It does in minutes what takes a forensics team hours or days to do," Wethers said as he tapped more keys.

"Yeah, but those guys sticking to the old methods score a lot closer to the original thing. This program can fill in the blanks, but it can't read the bone beneath the flesh to recreate scars that might have been there. We'll miss out on a lot of positive IDs because of that.''

"Yeah, but we'll be in the ballpark, buddy, and right now that's the place we need to be."

A hologram pad to Wethers's left blossomed into life. A rainbow explosion of colors erupted into the air, starting six inches above the pad. Then they melted and ran together. When it came into focus, a floating three-dimensional representation of the face on the monitor hung in the air. It was only sixty percent of the original head's size.

Wethers tapped the keyboard.

Obediently the hologram started a slow full-circle, moving endlessly. Every feature was in place, human. But the eyes looked as though anthracite had been placed behind the half-closed lids.

The computer's hard drive whirred. Kurtzman knew another facet of the program had booted up. Computer-generated pictures were being taken of the floating head from every conceivable angle and stored in a file separate from the others Wethers had already worked on.

"Every time I see this," Wethers said as he watched the program run, "I can't help but think about those damn voodoo movies we used to watch as kids— zombies, shrunken heads, hell, the works. Sometimes this stuff scares the bejesus out of me. All afternoon I've felt like I'm supposed to sacrifice a chicken after each face I put back together."

Wethers tapped another combination of keys. The head evaporated from the hologram pad, starting at the scalp and flowing down to the jagged neckline. He turned in his chair and raised his voice. "Carmen."

The woman seated across the room swiveled to face him. Carmen Delahunt was petite and vivacious. But her red hair was a distinct warning not to cross over on to her bad side. She was every inch the professional, having served fifteen years with the FBI at Quantico before Hal Brognola stole her away. "You've got another one?"

"It's in your file."

"Thanks." Efficient as always, Delahunt turned back to her screen and her own sleuth work. Her fingers worked the keyboard rapidly.

Wethers returned to his own board and punched in a fresh series of commands. The monitor quickly filled with another face. This one's skull was laid open like a fan of orange sections. Wethers sucked on his pipe in renewed enthusiasm. "This," he said in a preoccupied voice, "could take some imagination on my part."

Kurtzman said, "If there's anything I can do, let me know." He rolled back from the workstation and across the large room to Delahunt.

Where Wethers's relationship with his keyboard was studious and methodical, Delahunt worked briskly and efficiently, going down the mental list of options she'd made for her search.

A new face—Arabic and middle-aged, with a thick black mustache and acne-scarred cheeks—popped onto her monitor. Another monitor, this one slaved to the first, flashed through a rapid search of CIA files, newspaper clippings from international papers and stills from television news footage.

"Anything you need here, Carmen?" Kurtzman asked.

"No, thanks, Aaron." Delahunt nodded toward the bank of telephones jacked into a row of modems hard-lined into the mainframe she was using. "I'm tied into the New York Library, Quantico and CBS's computerized news service. Occasionally I get a lead that takes me somewhere else, but a lot of the jobbing is coming straight from there."

"Any luck?"

"So far I'm hitting about forty percent. That's not bad, but I've got some other stuff on tap that might boost that figure. You're getting my best."

"Never doubted that for a minute, lady."

She smiled.

On-screen the flat hologram image of the terrorist shifted to a one-quarter profile, then tilted slightly down. The monitor split, and the pixels on the right side flashed, then gathered into a black-and-white picture of a mob scene.

Delahunt tapped the keyboard, and the mob picture blew up six sizes. A livid red circle etched around the face of the man held forcibly between two Egyptian policemen. A caption at the bottom referred to a hotel bombing in Cairo three years earlier.

Delahunt blew the picture up a few more sizes.

There was no doubt in Kurtzman's mind that this was the man they were searching for.

Working diligently, Delahunt programmed in the date, place and incident. The hard drive whirred and clicked. The images faded from the monitor and were replaced by sections of newsprint. *Time* listed the details. Evidently a small group of the May 15 Organization had broken into the Aladdin Continental Motel and set bombs that killed the owner, Lyron Mandy, and seventeen of his staff. Nine guests were also killed in the explosions. Four of them were vacationing Americans. The news team covering the bombing was told by an unidentified caller that the May 15 Organization had executed Mandy as an example to the other Zionist supporters who regularly sent large amounts of their earnings to the Israeli government to field terrorist teams against the Palestinians.

Delahunt tapped in a shorthand line of symbols after scanning the article.

A few seconds later a CIA file opened up regarding Agency involvement in the investigation. Four pages into the computer-generated document, there was another picture of the terrorist, as well as a brief bio.

"His name was Rafi Aqaba," Delahunt said. Her hands moved across the keyboard, tied in the new information to the picture. "He was a member of the May 15 Organization until at least the fall of last year, when he was seen fleeing the scene of an attempted kidnapping of an American businessman in Syria.''

A window opened up below a frontal shot of Aqaba and listed terrorist activity the man had been tied to and was presently wanted for. It included hints of other operations the CIA had put together from informants.

Kurtzman read it. Aqaba had seemed to have covered the gamut: shootings, stabbings, bombings and hijackings. The man had certainly had his act down pat, at least until he'd crossed paths with Able Team.

He murmured appreciative encouragement and went on to visit briefly with the last member of his present team.

Akira Tokaido was the youngest of Kurtzman's cybernetic specialists, and by far the most abrasive. The computer in Tokaido's hands wasn't a tool; it was an extension of his mind. Kurtzman couldn't follow some of the younger man's leaps of logic, but Tokaido's results were unimpeachable. But as great as those successes sometimes were, so were the failures.

As usual, Tokaido had a mini-CD player plugged into one ear, and his lips moved with the words of the heavy metal song grinding into his brain. His shock of black hair was also shocking in an ultramodern hairstyle.

"What have you got for me?" Kurtzman asked. He rolled to a stop and studied the three monitors arranged in front of Tokaido.

"A growing list of ID clearing houses for our friends, the terrorists," Tokaido said nonchalantly.

Though the young man's tone was light, Kurtzman knew Tokaido was committed to the task laid before them.

"Even though none of these guys were carrying any ID," Tokaido went on as he worked the keyboard, "after Carmen tags 'em with a name, I can go back to their last known residences in CIA and Mossad files and move them transglobally toward here. By finding out where their real names disappeared, I can back-track on the information their pictures turned up in legit visas granted through the State Department."

"Surprising how many of them can fall through the cracks, isn't it?" Kurtzman asked.

"Oh, yeah. You got bankers listed in here who don't look like they know what a time-lock safe is. You got architects who look like they'd be more accustomed to an AK-47 than a slide rule. You'd think somebody along the line would have wised up to these jokers."

"Appearances can be deceiving."

"If you ask me, a little common sense would have worked wonders when the visa people just looked at the passport photos."

"What about the paper on the terrorists?"

"Finest stuff you can get your hands on. Confidentially I don't think we could do much better from our end."

"Got a source?"

"East Coast definitely. Maybe New York, New Jersey. Somewhere in there. I've looked at enough paper coming out of Florida and the southern environs for the Colombians to know in my gut it's not those guys. I don't figure West Coast because some of the people I've been able to track have made connections in France and West Germany. That puts them basically in another hemisphere. It would have been a different story if I'd found their trails in Singapore and Hong Kong."

"Right."

"When I get the specs and a pretty good guess as to who's handling the details, I'll get with you."

"Good enough. Any guess as to how many terrorists have slipped through?"

"I've got Intel coming in from the State Department now. The oldest visa I identified on one of the known terrorists has been five months. It was expired, and he was on Immigration's files, but they hadn't caught up with him. I'm adding a couple months just to be on the safe side, then downloading all the visas State issued to anyone from the Middle East during that time. After that it'll be a matter of elimination. Some will show up immediately like the guy I mentioned who jumped out of sight once his visa expired. I can catch others who're over here on work or school visas by checking with job sites and universities. The flow of monies will red-flag others. But any way you look at it, Aaron, you're looking at a project that's going to take time."

"When you start getting this stuff in, break it down and get back with me periodically. We'll parcel it out to some of the staff and let some of the outside agencies help us comb through the files. It'll give us a chance to get it down quicker."

Tokaido nodded and focused on the bank of monitors again.

Finally noticing the headache that had crept up on him, Kurtzman wheeled back to his end of the room. It was okay to touch base with his people, to let them know he was there if they needed him. It was another to waste their time.

Back at his desk he popped two painkillers, then tapped in a quick code and snared a satellite line from CNN. His monitor blinked, then the image of the news anchor came on. Two retired military analysts swapped theories as the female anchor tried to regain control over the interview.

The general consensus seemed to be that another Middle Eastern war loomed on the horizon for the American people.

Kurtzman didn't know that he agreed with that yet, but it was for damn sure shaping up to be one hell of a shoot-out.

KHALID SHAWIYYA GRIPPED the butt of the nickel-plated Detonics Combat Master .45 ACP holstered on his right hip and gave it a reassuring squeeze. He'd acquired the weapon only hours ago, and it would take time for him to become accustomed to it. Pride still swelled in him. He thought it was truly a fine weapon for the president and commander in chief of Iraq. It beat the hell out of the Soviet handguns he'd been offered, and it dramatically offset the solid black military uniform he'd chosen for this night's schedule.

He was thick and blocky, with a stomach that stubbornly persisted in being paunchy no matter how much he exercised. But the tailors who'd designed his uniform had hidden that imperfection as well as anyone could who was under the threat of death.

His face was rectangular and hard-edged. Once he'd heard it compared to the working end of a military trenching tool. Then he'd killed, with his own bare hands, the man who made the comparison. His thick black mustache was carefully trimmed under his proudly hooked nose.

He studied his reflection in the mirror of his ready room and was satisfied. He was a man to be feared, a man who could run this country despite the fumbled attempts of the coward Saddam Hussein.

Hussein had feared to throw all the combined might of his terrorist organizations against the United States. In the end the man had been afraid for his own life. That was the reason Hussein had abdicated his office at the quiet insistence of the Arab Ba'ath Socialist Party. None of them would suffer to have a broken man leading them on their divine quest.

"President Shawiyya," an aide's voice called from behind him. "You wanted me to remind you when it was time, sir."

"Thank you, Ahkeel. I'll be joining you momentarily."

The door closed.

He reached for the hat rack outside the walk-through closet of his ready room, selected one of the dozen black berets hanging there and placed it on his head at what he thought was a jaunty angle. He pulled on a pair of black calfskin gloves with cut-out palms, straightened the tunic with its impressive cluster of medals and moved for the door.

Two lines of his Republican Guards snapped to attention at once.

He walked past them, no man daring to meet his eye. He didn't glance at the videocamera station he'd had built on a platform on the wall to his right. The technicians there would have the tape rolling or they'd be dead before the sun rose the next morning. They had instructions to get some good shots of the Detonics on his hip.

The presidential palace had suffered great destruction from the American bombs, and it had been rebuilt according to his specifications.

The reception room had a ten-foot ceiling in a forty-by-forty area. It had to be big. He'd ordered all Iraqi newspapers and television stations to have representatives here. It was white and very plain. There were no windows because of the threat of snipers.

He gazed out at the audience and smiled benignly. It was a smile he'd practiced in the mirror. He waved. Many of the dozens of people crowded into the room waved back. The presidential camera crew had instructions to catch that, as well.

A long wooden table occupied one end of the room under a bank of lights designed to promote a high quality of photography. It was simple, unadorned, the kind of furniture the peasants and lower-class citizens would have in their homes. That way they could see that he lived as simply as they did, that they fought for the same things against the Europeans who would keep them economically, politically and religiously repressed if they could. The chairs had been constructed in the same fashion.

He sat and waved his hand.

The people who had been previously notified of their selection to join him at the table came forward. He took note of the people who didn't seem totally enamored of the great gift they'd been given.

One of the first at the table was Hadleigh Jonas, the British CNN correspondent. The man was slim, dapper, but his eyes showed the strain of having been up the past twenty or more hours. Six more people followed. Shawiyya knew the names of most of them, but regarded none of them as highly as the CNN reporter. Jonas could relay a message heard halfway around the world.

A cluster of microphones was quickly set up on the tabletop until it looked like an electronic flower arrangement.

"Please begin," Shawiyya ordered.

"Mr. President," Jonas said from the opposite end of the table, "were you involved in the attack on the United Nations base in Kuwait City?"

"Yes. Special forces under my direction were ordered to perform the attack. But only on the bases held by the United States personnel."

"But it was my understanding that several Kuwaiti, British and French military personnel were killed in that attack, as well."

Shawiyya spread his hands. "Such are the vagaries of war."

"You feel no remorse?"

"No. None. When the Americans dropped their so-called SMART bombs in our country, were these bombs intelligent enough to strike only the guilty? No. Civilians died in those explosions. Women and children. The United States paints itself as pristine, as having no blood on its hands. It *does* have blood on its hands—Iraqi blood. And it will be avenged."

On cue, the audience gave roaring vent to its approval of Shawiyya's statement.

"The United States and its President have continued to make war on my country despite the concessions made after the last war. They influenced the Kurds to revolt, to promote inner strife in a country already reeling under their famed high-tech weapons. They have become the aggressor in this new conflict. I'm merely picking up the gauntlet they have thrown down."

"And you believe that is the situation you are facing here?"

"Yes. For the past year the United States has been fighting an undeclared war against my country. My predecessor was a victim of defamation of character. So much of what was printed or told about him was untrue. If he was the black-hearted villain the Americans labeled him to be, he would have never given up the fight. He'd have fought them until his dying breath."

"But he's gone now."

"Yes. He was a coward, and he took the coward's way out." Shawiyya slammed his clenched fist against the tabletop. "But I'm made of sterner stuff than Saddam Hussein." He flung both arms wide. "The people of this country are made of sterner stuff than Saddam Hussein. They have tolerated all of the Americans' efforts to foment insurrection in their homeland they care to. We won't take it any longer."

"What can you tell me about the attack on the Persian Gulf War Memorial in Washington, D.C.?"

"Agents acting under my orders blew that sham away. There was no American victory. Our people's heads were bowed by a traitor to our beliefs. The Arab world was once the epitome of strength and unity. We've let ourselves be torn asunder by the American Satans and their allies. But we're reforming. We shall be whole again. Israel shall be blotted from the map. Whatever sacrifice we have to make, it shall be made. We'll have a return to greatness. We *will* have unity."

A thunderous and savage approval shot through the chamber. Men and women screamed in what sounded like ecstasy.

Shawiyya kept his face impassive through an act of willpower. His body sang with almost sexual urgency. He realized he'd been born for this position, had been born to lead his people to the glory they so richly deserved.

"What about the high-tech weapons the Americans have?" Jonas asked when the clamor had subsided to a tolerable degree.

"Those weapons will only work if the American people have the heart to use them," Shawiyya replied. He made a claw of his right hand and slowly closed it. "I intend to rip that heart out. The Americans are a fearful people. They have quiet lives and quiet jobs. None of them has ever had to struggle as hard to take life from the world as the Iraqi people have had to struggle. My country, my people, we aren't afraid of the struggle."

More cheers echoed his words.

"For years the United States ignored Iraqi ties to what they considered to be terrorist groups. They did this because they then supported us in our efforts against Iran. When we were successful in our war, they grew to fear us. We were more powerful than they were ready to accept. The United States has gone to lengths to assure themselves there is no real strength in the Middle East. They've arranged to aid one Arab brother to fight against another. But it's time to put all that behind us. The United States might have their missiles and warplanes, but we of the Middle East have our secret weapon, too. The Americans try to evoke world sympathy by calling that weapon terrorism and painting an evil picture of it. But if a man comes at you with a gun and all you have is a rock, will you not use that rock to crush his skull to defend your way of life?''

A resounding ''yes'' shook the walls.

''I don't call these men terrorists,'' Shawiyya continued. ''I call them dedicated men. They are valorous. They don't shy away from giving their lives for their countries so that the Middle East and the Arab world will have the future the United States and her allies try so desperately to deny us. They've become nations of users, of takers. And they see us as the people and nations they can take from. The discovery of oil in our countries started to pull us onto an economic level with them. They couldn't abide this. They don't want to lose their superpower status. Just as the British didn't want to lose Iraq as a supplier of their natural resources and plunge into an economic abyss they so deserved.''

There was a moment of silence after the cheering died away.

Hadleigh Jonas met Shawiyya's glance full measure.

Shawiyya was pleased. The man had been well-schooled for the interview.

"But," Jonas said in a quiet voice, "by taking this stance, you realize you're setting yourself up as a target for the retaliatory efforts of the United States."

"Yes. I do understand this. I've treated them as I would treat any enemy—I've killed them where I've found them. I intend to find more of them and kill more of them. At least I'm being more honest about my war against them than they've been in their tactics against my country." Shawiyya paused for effect. "And even if I become a target as you say, I rejoice in that. Even the Americans—despite their vaunted high-tech weaponry—cannot stand against a united Arab republic." He waved his hands toward himself. "Let them come to take me. It'll save me the trouble of going after them!"

MACK BOLAN SNAPPED OFF the jeep's public broadcast radio in disgust, cutting Khalid Shawiyya off in midsentence. There was no satisfaction. He sat in the passenger seat with his weapons from the raid to free the hostages packed in a duffel at his feet. Visions of what the Iraqi president was planning hammered at his mind relentlessly.

The hot tarmac of the military airstrip hadn't cooled with the coming of night yet. Heat waves shimmered up, fired by starlight and security lamps. The sound of helicopters and fighter jets taking off and landing echoed over the flat plains stretching out on all four sides of the airport. The tower stood in front of them like a fat finger pointing toward the full moon.

"Something wrong, sir?" the driver asked.

"Nothing to do with your driving, Corporal," Bolan said.

"Yes, sir."

They wheeled around the rows of fighting aircraft. Kept separate for the most part, the American planes were mixed in with the French, Saudi Arabian, British, Italian and Kuwaiti air forces. All bore the logo of the United Nations peacekeeping forces.

Foot patrols overseeing airport security were at a maximum. UN MP jeeps crossed the tarmac restlessly.

Minutes later they arrived at Jack Grimaldi's borrowed Harrier. The pilot prowled restlessly outside his craft. He was dressed in dark clothing with a Colt Government .45 in side leather and an M-16 slung over his shoulder. When he saw the jeep approaching, he shadowed his eyes with a hand, then dropped his cigarette, crushed it underfoot and took his bomber jacket from the wing.

The jeep halted in front of the fighter jet.

"Colonel Pollock."

Bolan leaped out of the jeep and looked back at the corporal.

"I just wanted to say thanks, sir. One of those men you brought back an hour ago, well, he was a good friend, sir. And sometimes it's a damn shame when thank-you doesn't seem enough."

Bolan smiled slightly and shook hands with the other man. "But it doesn't come any better in this man's Army, Corporal. Carry on."

The driver saluted smartly and drove off.

Bolan hoisted his duffel over his shoulder and approached Grimaldi. The pilot was an old friend, scarred from some of the same wars as the Executioner. They'd both found their beginnings in Vietnam, and Fate had reunited them during the Mafia wars.

"Rough one from what I hear," Grimaldi said as he led the way to the plane.

"There aren't going to be any cakewalks in this one, Jack."

"Yeah. I get that feeling, too. Did you get a chance to listen to the radio?"

The warrior nodded. "Some."

Grimaldi gave him a quick rundown on the events that had ensnared Phoenix Force and Able Team in the same hours Bolan had been working to free the hostages.

"Sounds too organized for Shawiyya," Bolan said when Grimaldi finished. "The man's only been in power a few months. Even if Saddam Hussein had the apparatus in place, getting the pin pulled wouldn't have happened this fast unless Shawiyya had a lot of backing."

"To hear the guy," Grimaldi said, "you'd think he's ready to take on the whole world with one arm tied behind his back. Come to think of it, things would probably be simpler if he did.''

Even as Bolan was assimilating the new Intel, getting acquainted with the idea that there were hundreds of civilians down in an operation that was only hours old, the first rocket exploded into the airfield less than a hundred yards away.

He raked the Walther MPK from the duffel bag he'd just tossed up into the open cockpit, then hunkered down beside the jet for cover. Grimaldi squatted with the M-16 across his knees only a few feet away.

More rockets pummeled the tarmac, smoking craters appearing in their wake.

Warning Klaxons shrilled into sudden life. Tracer fire erupted from ground units, and green arcs cut through the night. More than a dozen shadows that blotted out the stars swept in from the northwest, seeming to follow the unbroken muzzle-flashes of 30 mm cannon.

A Huey Cobra mushroomed into a ball of flame and showered bits of fiery wreckage over the airfield. The helicopter's corpse landed twisted and bent among a squad of F-16 fighters. A triple burst of explosions threw a concussive force wave over the airstrip that took out another handful of jets, and an inferno whirled from the scattered aircraft. Men in flight suits pushed themselves up from the ground to help others and run for safety.

''Mack, look!''

Bolan followed the pointing line of Grimaldi's arm. Along the east wall an army seemed to rise up out of the darkness of the desert. Two hundred yards out, nothing separated them from the airstrip but a ten-foot-high chain-link fence.

The low-flying jets thundered overhead.

"Mirages," Grimaldi said as they passed. "Outdated F-1s, but they're enough to get the job done. And they've got Soviet MiG-29s running backup."

Out on the runway an F-4G Wild Weasel tried to get airborne. Before its wheels more than left the tarmac, one of the MiG-29s swooped over the Weasel and put an air-to-air missile through its spine. The Weasel fireballed and spread out over the runway.

"Goddamn it," Grimaldi said with feeling. He tossed the M-16 into the cockpit of the Harrier and clambered after it.

Thirty mm cannonfire beat hell out of the airstrip. Air-to-surface missiles took out ground targets in sychronized volleys, and the command tower went down in a pile of crumbling brick. A sheet of flame fully forty feet in height spread out behind an attacking Mirage after it scored a hit on the fuel depot.

"I'm getting up there," Grimaldi growled.

"Throw my duffel down," Bolan replied.

The pilot tossed down the bag, clamped a helmet and headset on, then lowered the canopy. The Harrier shivered as the jet engines roared to life.

Bolan was already in motion, driving his legs hard against the asphalt surface as he raced toward the fence. Grimaldi's natural element was the air. The Executioner's lay in the trenches. He shrugged into his gear as he ran, kept the duffel bag with him until he could transfer the spare clips to the web belts.

The sky was a roiling hornet's nest that scattered edged silhouettes across the face of the moon. A last glance over the warrior's shoulder showed Grimaldi's Harrier taking off vertically. The jet looked like an ungainly duck slowly leaping into the air, then it swirled out into the occupied airspace like a hunting falcon.

UN ground forces converged on the east side of the airfield. Mortar fire from the attacking terrorists fell among man, machines and landscape indiscriminately. Jeeps and M-998 HMMWVs screeched around burning airplanes.

A mortar round whistled overhead, landed twenty yards to Bolan's left, directly in the path of a jeep. The explosion caught the vehicle in a whip-snap like a terrier's jaws closing after an elusive fly. The jeep went airborne, tumbled end over end and came down hard.

The Executioner changed course. When he got to the jeep there was nothing he could do for the two Marines wedged under it. But he picked up the M-249 Squad Automatic Weapon lying near it and slid it into the shoulder bag of extra magazines.

Less than twenty men had made it to the fence to face the approaching army of terrorists. Most of them were outfitted only with small arms.

The Executioner clambered to the top of an overturned ten-wheeler lying next to the fence. He took up a position across the side of the truck cab, extended the SAW's bipod and clicked off the safety. He worked the weapon in a series of long bursts that chopped through the ranks of the onrushing Arabs.

The 5.56 mm rounds accounted for heavy casualties the front line. It only slowed the lines behind them slightly as they stepped over the bodies.

As he changed the first 200-round magazine for another, Bolan could hear the fierce yelling of the approaching terrorists. He knew they were *fedayeen* and willing to die in the attack.

Bullets scarred and punctured the truck cab before Bolan opened up with the second magazine. In the periphery of his vision he saw one of the UN soldiers go spinning away from the fence. The Executioner rode the SAW hard, conscious of the way the sweeps got longer when the terrorists got closer.

The clank of tank treads sounded low and ominous. There were three of them, almost abreast with the front line of terrorists now.

The Executioner fired again and again, tried to make every bullet count.

The whoosh of a rocket nearby sounded just before a warhead impacted against the turret of the tank on the left. The turret came apart. The tank rocked to a halt, smoke pouring from the interior. The other tanks continued to fire, lobbing 115 mm shells into the ranked United Nations aircraft. The rate of fire was slow but constant.

Without warning, a flaming jet slammed into the ground behind the advancing line of terrorists.

As the two surviving tanks neared the fence, some of the *fedayeen* climbed on board. When the tanks rolled up against the fence, the terrorists threw themselves over the barbed wire and landed on the UN forces.

Bolan almost cut one of the terrorists in two with a sweep of the SAW. Then the weapon clicked dry as three more men charged toward him.

5

Mack Bolan pushed himself to his feet as the human tide threatened to overwhelm him. He reversed the empty SAW, because there was no time to draw another weapon, and swung. Flesh crumpled under the blow, and fresh blood warmed his hands. His breath came hard and tight into his lungs. Two bullets, maybe more, bounced from his Kevlar vest with bruising impacts. He targeted the gunner, hooked the metal buttstock of the SAW into the terrorist and destroyed his lower face. The man went flying backward, ending up hung in the barbed wire topping the fence.

He kicked another terrorist in the crotch with his boot. The scream was inhuman, penetrating the loss of hearing the sheer overload of sounds had caused. He grabbed the SAW by the barrel and cleared a path through the terrorists.

Leaping from the overturned ten-wheeler, he rolled and came up on his feet with the Desert Eagle in his fist. The big .44 bucked, and another Arab went down. He ducked under a knife, put a pair of 240-grain rounds through the blade wielder's lungs.

The Executioner ran through the clip firing point-blank at his assailants. Movement became automatic, as natural as breathing, fired solely by the need to survive.

The two terrorist tanks, Soviet T-62s, rolled into the airstrip over dead men, their 115 mm main guns hammering out irregular thunder.

Bolan grabbed the pistol arm of a last attacker, slammed the guy's jaw with the SAW and shoved him under the closest tank tread. The Arab didn't have enough time to scream before the forty-ton tank erased recognizable humanity from his corpse.

Reaching over his shoulder, the Executioner drew the Mossberg Bullpup 12 from its rigging across his back. In two strides he was even with the T-62. He fired the shotgun from the hip as the coaxial gunner spotted him and started to come around. The double-ought buck plucked the gunner from his station and left the 7.62 mm machine gun untenanted.

Then Bolan was on board. He removed a grenade from his webbing, pulled the pin, yanked the turret hatch open and dropped the bomb inside. He triggered two rounds from the Mossberg through the hatch to keep the crew too busy to look for the grenade, which went off a couple of seconds later. The tank clanked to a halt.

Fifty yards farther on, the second tank came into contact with an air-to-surface missile that destroyed it.

The tank Bolan had disabled absorbed the brunt of the blast. Flying shrapnel cut his cheek and arm.

An Arab leaped at him from the small crowd gathered behind the tank. The Executioner fired from a distance of three feet. The shotgun charge punched the corpse away. He fired the Mossberg dry, reloaded and went on.

A haze of blue cordite smoke swirled over the airfield. Whirling cherries of rescue vehicles seemed like beacons in an ocean of death. Suddenly there were no more terrorists.

Bolan stepped over the body of the last man he'd gunned down and found himself looking into the surprised faces of the UN soldiers. He glanced into the sky, saw that allied forces owned that, as well. Whatever Mirages and MiGs had been up there were gone now.

He wiped his face tiredly, amazed at the amount of blood covering him that wasn't his own.

Hard-eyed men began the task of sorting through the dead to find the living. If there'd been any amateurs before the battle, only professional warriors remained standing. Their faces held the look. He ran into Jack Grimaldi on his third trip into the makeshift medical center for the severely wounded. This was the second time he'd made it in with a man who'd lived long enough for the base doctors to take over.

The Stony Man pilot looked drawn and haggard. A cut with a dried trickle of blood frozen down his temple glinted darkly in the high-intensity lighting.

An hour later the life-and-death cleanup of the airfield had been finished. They stopped long enough for cups of coffee some enterprising individual had arranged, then headed back to Grimaldi's borrowed Harrier.

The fighter jet was no longer unmarked. Bullet holes peppered the hull, but Grimaldi pronounced it airworthy. Clearance for takeoff was granted immediately. A temporary tower post had been set up, but there was precious little in the way of air traffic to oversee.

The damage to the airstrip looked even worse from above. Bolan asked Grimaldi to circle twice while he took it all in. Fires still burned in different areas. Occasionally an explosion would spread a new pool of smoke and flame. The UN barracks bases were to the southeast. Neither installation was outfitted to repel another terrorist attack. A defensive posture would gain nothing here, and the Executioner knew it. Stony Man Farm lay ten hours away by the time they made their transport changes and fueling stops. That made it at least a day, not counting the briefing that Kurtzman, Price and Brognola would deliver, before he could return.

A lot could happen in a day. A lot could happen in an hour. He'd just seen an allied stronghold turned into rubble. He leaned his head back in the seat and closed his eyes for just a moment.

Grimaldi kicked in the afterburners, and the G-force pushed them back in the seats. The pilot's voice crackled in Bolan's ear over the radio. "Feel like that old George Carlin joke,'' Grimaldi said. ''About hurrying up to go so you can get back.''

Bolan nodded. He knew exactly what the pilot was talking about.

"STRIKER'S EN ROUTE," Barbara Price announced when she hung up the phone. ''The UN airbase in Kuwait City is almost entirely out of commission. It'll be days before they're up to forty percent efficiency for possible retaliatory air strikes against Iraq. And that's if they aren't attacked again. The USS *Theodore Roosevelt* is standing by in the gulf to give air support if necessary, but all they can provide is a defensive posture.''

Hal Brognola gave a tight nod while he continued to stare through the one-way glass overlooking the interrogation room where Wael Boudia paced the floor restlessly. It—like the observation room—was normally a bedroom, if in use at all. Now it held only a small table, a folding chair and a television-computer monitor combo built into the wall so it couldn't be removed.

During the slack times Price and Kurtzman were the only permanent residents of the Farm. She ran a hand through her tousled blond hair. Her plastic container of orange juice had perspired and left a wet circle on a stack of computer printouts she'd studied earlier. She took a sip, then lifted the phone, punched an inside number and peered through the one-way glass.

Boudia was a slender, good-looking man with a neatly trimmed mustache. In tennis whites he could have passed for a professional tennis player. He looked younger than the thirty-four years that was listed on his bio. Dressed in crisp, ironed stone-wash jeans and an open-throated black-and-white silk pullover, he looked like a man with no worries. Gold gleamed at his neck, both wrists and a couple fingers. For a one-time terrorist who'd abandoned Saddam Hussein because of the barbaric acts he'd been asked to perform, Boudia seemed to have done well by himself.

The phone was answered on the second ring. "Kurtzman."

"It's me," Price said. "Are you about ready to start the floor show?"

"Just buzz me from inside the room. I'll handle the displays and recordings myself."

Price said thanks and hung up. She drained her orange juice, but her throat still felt dry. She wished there was time to go to her room, get out of the jeans and blouse she'd been in for the past sixteen hours and take a long, hot shower. She was pushing herself too hard and she knew it, but she didn't know how to back off.

Lifting one leg at a time, she squeezed back into the cowboy boots that had been pinching her feet. It had been a relief to get them off for the time it took her to review Boudia's files and oversee the exfiltration of the Stony Man teams and Striker. Able Team was already on base, standing down with Leo Turrin and Cowboy

John Kissinger while Kurtzman and his people reeled in the information they so desperately needed.

"You ready?" she asked Brognola.

The big Fed turned to face her. "Yeah. But I can handle this by myself if you want to grab ten."

"So can I," she said with more edge than she'd intended. "You were only invited as a courtesy." She caught herself at the door, one hand on the knob. She exhaled. "I'm sorry, Hal. I didn't mean for it to come out like that."

"It's okay, kiddo. We're all working under a strain here. We both have a habit of trying to shoulder the bulk of responsibility. Gets kind of sticky when we both reach for the same hunk of responsibility."

She turned to him, kissed him lightly on the cheek, more intimate than she'd been in all the years that she'd known him. He held her for just a moment, somehow knowing that was what she needed.

Breaking out of his embrace, she took the lead, Boudia's Justice Department folder clasped tightly in her hand.

A black-uniformed Stony Man security guard holding an H&K MP-5 stood to one side of the locked door. He nodded curtly as Price took out a key for the door and opened it. His weapon was lowered into the ready position as Price and Brognola stepped into the room.

Boudia started to say something, then saw the menacing barrel of the H&K. He raised his hands and backed away. Fear and anger pinched white lines around his thin-lipped mouth. "Hey, what the hell is this? Now you're going to take me out and shoot me?"

The Stony Man guard retreated from the room. The lock clicked hollowly.

"Have a seat, Mr. Boudia," Price said. Out of the corner of her eye she saw Brognola set up camp near the doorway. Wanting to intimidate the man as much as she could in as short a time as possible, Price moved to the other end of the room.

Boudia was stranded in the middle.

Knowing the value of a faceless threat, Price stood with her back to the room's only window. There was no glass pane. Instead, the window was filled with two inches of an acrylic composite that was not only bulletproof but would also take an enormous amount of damage from a battering ram before caving in. The afternoon sun was setting on this side of the main house. She knew she'd be framed by the sunlight, her features left blurred and indistinct.

Boudia stared at her, then shifted his gaze to Brognola.

The big Fed's face was impassive as he took a cigar from a pocket inside his jacket. The flash of the 10 mm Delta Elite was deliberate. He unwrapped the cigar with calm deliberation and stuck the stogie into a corner of his mouth. "The lady said to have a seat."

Fumbling, Boudia reached behind him and pulled the folding chair into place. He sat behind the small table as if it was some kind of barrier. "You can't do this to me. I have rights. I'm under the protection of the United States government.''

Brognola crossed the room in a measured stride. He leaned down and placed his hands flat on the table-top, his face inches from Boudia's.

Price could tell from the surge of fear in Boudia's liquid brown eyes that whatever security he'd drawn from having the table between himself and them had evaporated.

''As of this moment,'' Brognola growled, ''you have no rights. Whatever rights you want, you'll have to earn.''

''You can't do that.'' Boudia appeared to be on the verge of explosion. ''I've already cooperated with the American government. I was promised a new life.''

''Now you're going to cooperate with us,'' Brognola said. ''There have been terrorist attacks against America and her allies in Kuwait City and Washington, D.C. Khalid Shawiyya has been on television threatening more to come. You're the only source we know of who can put us close to what's going on in that country. You *will* cooperate.''

''I don't know anything more than I've already told the CIA.''

''I don't believe you. When you were picked up by federal marshals, you were packing a bag to go. And you had the money to go with. That leads me to think there's something you haven't shared with us.''

"Shawiyya is someone other than Saddam Hussein," Boudia said desperately. "I was an expert on Saddam's policies and practices, not Shawiyya's."

"Yeah, well, I have trouble believing a whole new terrorist network has gone into operation since you've been gone."

Boudia glanced quickly in Price's direction. His eyes held a silent plea.

Price knew from the man's files that Boudia was something of an accomplished ladies' man. And his taste ran to American blondes. Keeping her arms folded over her breasts, she smiled sweetly, figuring the guy was going for the good-cop-bad-cop routine.

"Before you left the May 15 Organization," Price said, "you were responsible for one hundred twenty-seven bombing deaths aboard an El Al flight three years ago. You participated in the assassination of three Mossad agents working undercover in Beirut fourteen months after that. Fifty-six more people died from the bomb you planted in a Paris bistro."

Boudia stared at her, his fingers pulling at his lips unconsciously.

"Need I go on?"

"No."

"You haven't been a nice guy," Price continued. "Nobody would miss you if you were to drop off the edge of the earth."

Silent, Boudia watched her as she walked closer, the way he would watch a snake readying itself to strike.

"Personally," Price said in an even voice, "I'm willing to gift wrap you for the Israelis and air-drop your ass into Tel Aviv with a toe tag already in place."

It was too bad there weren't any good cops in the room.

"YOU'VE OVERSTATED your cause, Shawiyya. You've tried to set yourself up as the champion of the Arab peoples. This is *not* what you were supposed to have done."

Khalid Shawiyya listened as the unidentifiable voice berated him over the telephone. He was in his private quarters below the presidential palace. Six Republican Guards stood at attention in the hallway outside his door. If by some slim chance an assassin got by them, there were still the four locks on the door, the secret passage inside the closet and—if need be—his Detonics. He caressed the pistol butt like the smooth flesh of a lover.

"You told me to get the attention of the Americans," Shawiyya said in his own defense. "I have done this."

"And tried to make yourself out to be the hero, as well." The voice snorted in derision. "Tread carefully, my brother, because I think you're following too closely in the footsteps of your mentor."

"Saddam Hussein was no hero."

"Neither are you." The tone in the mystery voice was mocking.

"The American people fear me."

"As they would fear a rabid dog."

Shawiyya remained silent with effort. At times it seemed he almost placed the voice. He couldn't recognize it from the timbre or nasal inflections. It was too carefully masked for that. But sometimes the word choice or the way sentences were put together jangled soft alarms inside his head. Memories coiled in the darkness of his mind.

"You're no savior to the Arab people," the voice went on. "You're but a man who wields power. If it were not you who succeeded Saddam as the president of Iraq, it would have been another."

"There was no other choice." Shawiyya clenched his fists in his rage.

"Sometimes I wonder if another might have behaved more reasonably than you. You place too much interest on personal glories and not enough on the future of the Middle East. You would have statues erected in your name. Already your name and face is more predominant than Saddam's. Your media is flooded with it. Architecture and sculptures reflect your image. Iraq has already worshiped at the clay feet of one would-be god. Do not lead her people down the path to doom by becoming another."

"You push me too far," Shawiyya said. His fingers coiled around the phone line. He wanted to rip it from the wall.

The voice laughed. "I lead you to greatness if you will listen, fool. But you won't come into the light."

"Nor do I live in hiding as you do."

"When the time is right, the world will know me."

"So you say."

"And it will *be* as I say." The voice paused. "There are a number of reasons why I don't reveal myself. With no central figure for the Americans or their allies to pursue, they'll spread their forces thin. They'll attempt to ferret out the strength behind the terrorist movement ravaging their homelands and their armies. In doing so they'll try to do as they've always done in the past—trample on the rights and dignities of the Arab people. They fear us. They fear our combined power. One man, they need not fear at all. The American President proved that when he used his war against Iraq to destroy the army and air force of your country rather than try to crush Saddam Hussein."

"Things are different now."

"Things are the same. If you continue to pursue your personal vanities, you'll end up as Saddam did."

Shawiyya licked his lips nervously. The rage was strong within him. "Perhaps the time will come when our goals no longer lie in the same direction."

"Perhaps it will. And if it does, you'll be dead before the next sun sets. I give you my promise on that. I won't have Saddam Hussein's folly replaced after all the sacrifice my people and I have made for the Arab community." The phone clicked dead.

Resisting the impulse to throw the phone set against the wall and smash it, Shawiyya hung it up instead and replaced it on the desk in the corner of the room. He shouted curses at the ceiling, then kicked his steel-toed boots through the elegant teak paneling lining the walls of the room.

A guard poked his head in through the door.

Shawiyya picked up a glass from the wet bar, threw it and roared, "Leave me alone, fool!"

A split second before the glass hit, the guard closed the door. Splintered shards dropped to the Persian rug and glinted in the recessed lighting.

Shawiyya hated himself because he was afraid. This unknown personage had become a part of his life over these past months since Saddam's abdication. Before, there'd been the whispered intimations that someone of power was taking an interest in him. Now the voice contacted him, told him what to do as if he were a servant.

So far it hadn't taken on the guise of a man. The owner of the voice lurked somewhere in the dark corners of the Middle East, and he controlled a large segment of the terrorist organizations Saddam Hussein had gathered back in the spring of 1990.

Shawiyya was certain he knew the man, but couldn't decide who it might be. He'd talked with the leaders of the other Arab countries, had conferred with King Hussein of Jordan, Kamal Majid, head of the pro-Iraqi groups in Egypt, Moammar Khaddafi in Libya, President Hafiz al-Assad of Syria, Iran's President Hashemi Rafsanjani and Yasser Arafat.

All of them knew of the voice. Most had heard and agreed that it must be one of their own. Legends had sprung up in the terrorist groups and in most of the

Arab countries about the powerful man who was coming to free the Middle East from the shackles of the Great Satans.

But no one knew him. At least, no one who knew him was telling.

Frustrated, Shawiyya grabbed his black beret and clamped it on his head. In the hallway his guards fell into step beside him. No one spoke.

Back in the room where he'd met with the journalists and television crews, there was only a small group of Iraqi soldiers standing guard over three individuals who were down on their knees before the raised dais the table and chairs sat on.

Shawiyya gestured.

A man who knew camera work sprang to the wall where the collection of videotaping machines were. He shouldered one, then moved in a circle to capture the scene being played out.

"These are the spies?" Shawiyya asked impatiently.

"Yes, Commander." The captain saluted smartly and extended a soiled packet.

Looking down at the trio on their knees, Shawiyya accepted the packet. "You admit you are spies?"

Two of them were men. One was in his fifties, the other younger one his son. The woman was the man's second wife, not the son's mother. Shawiyya remembered this from the reports he'd been given.

"No, President Shawiyya," the old man answered. He glanced up fearfully, his hands crossed protectively over the top of his head. "I beg of you. I don't know how these monies came to be in my home. We have had nothing to do with the Americans. Please. We're innocents."

Shawiyya used the man's words against him. "So," he said, waving the packet around, "it's the American's money that has tempted you to turn against your country and your people."

"No, not the Americans."

"Then who? The Israelis?"

The man sobbed and bent down with his forehead touching the floor.

"You said you had nothing to do with the Americans. How did you know I was aware of your dealings with them?"

"I just assumed. You have attacked the Americans. I thought you suspected us of talking to them."

"You are pathetic," Shawiyya screamed. He tore the packet open and scattered the Iraqi bills over the kneeling trio like a paper snowstorm. He saved half of it, waved the cameraman to another position, then scattered more money so it could be taken from another angle and edited in later. He continued. "You sell out your country and your people to the Great Satans, yet you beg for your life. How many Iraqi lives do you think you have sold them with the information you have delivered, spy?"

"Please. I don't know—"

"You don't know? Perhaps, then, you'll tell me how much you got for those uncountable lives."

The man continued to sob and shook his head.

"You're a dog," Shawiyya screamed. "Even the Kurds know greater honor than you. They declare their enmity for me openly and bear arms in their defense."

With a snarl of rage, the young man threw himself forward.

His hand already on the butt of the Detonics .45, Shawiyya drew and fired. Three rounds drilled through the young man's chest. Shawiyya used both hands to push the bloody corpse from him while the echoes of the shots slowly died in the cavernous room.

The old man reached for his son, touched his face with a trembling hand. Tears splashed onto the younger man's crimson-smeared chest. The woman tried to console her husband in a voice that broke frequently.

"There's only one way to deal with spies," Shawiyya said, "and I don't mind if I have to do the job myself."

He deliberately aimed the pistol at the backs of the bowed heads, then fired two shots into each. Their bodies tumbled one atop the other.

Gazing down at them for a moment, he turned his face up to the camera. He curled a fist up and shook it at the lens. "The Americans try to poison us against each other. They seek to keep the Arab world split where we cannot stand against them. If you know of spies who are selling us out, don't hesitate to take justice into your own hands and seek these people out. They must die so that we can be strong."

He made a cutting gesture.

The cameraman stopped the film and popped the cassette out.

"Put that in my office and inform Daweesh I'll be there within the hour to put a final edit on the film. I want this tape playing on all of Iraqi television and CNN by sunrise."

"Yes, Commander."

Shawiyya reloaded his pistol as he walked away from the corpses. "Captain."

"Yes, sir."

"Have your men dispose of these bodies and clean up the blood. I'll be addressing the media again in the morning. I want this place in order."

"It will be as you say, Commander."

The Republican Guards followed him to the exit, then up the short flight of stairs to the balcony overlooking the exotic garden below. A guard stepped forward and opened the balcony doors. Another spoke briefly on a walkie-talkie.

"Everything is clear, sir," the guard announced after a moment.

Shawiyya moved out onto the balcony. He breathed in the fresh scents of the orange trees and date palm trees. Flowers of myriad hues grew in carefully controlled wild abandon. Oriental cabbages were ranked in squat, colorful formation. The garden was a thing of beauty, yet he'd never walked there. It was too un-protected, too open.

He glanced at his watch, checked the time and found there were only two minutes to go. With his hands together behind his back, he waited patiently.

Then, to the south, the event started taking shape. A cloud of illumination gathered less than a hundred yards above the city. Laser lights—burning electric blue, tangerine orange, red the hue of rubies, lemon yellow—shot through the sky.

He leaned on the balcony railing, watched the group that had gathered outside the presidential gates. An army of soldiers held them at bay. Behind them, masked by the shadows of night, the bombed husk of much of the city remained. No one had questioned the need to rebuild the presidential palace after Saddam Hussein's abdication. No one dared. The rest of the city would come later, as profits from the proposed Arab-dominated subcontinent rose from the ashes of Iraq.

The voices of the gathered crowd swelled. Surprise was in there, as well as adulation.

Shawiyya smiled. He'd been accepted by his people long ago. The voice on the phone refused to acknowl-edge the power he truly wielded. He knew it for what it was, and he anticipated its use.

A palate of rainbow-colored lights shone in the night. Then the colors blended in a dizzying fashion. In the space of a few heartbeats, Shawiyya's face ap-peared against the backdrop of the star-dappled night.

It was a stoic image of him that held the look of a leader. His black beret was briefly defined, crowned by the fires of distant suns. It wavered and changed to the image of the new flag he'd designed.

Cheers broke from the crowd at the gates, obviously led by the soldiers.

In the distance Shawiyya imagined he could hear others crying out joyously, as well.

He felt good, invincible. The Americans would find out the extent of his power in due time. When he was done with them, he'd turn his attention to the owner of the voice that had bedeviled him these past few months. He'd never willingly relinquish control of his country.

And another thought had been in his mind of late. The owner of this all-knowing voice had set himself up to come in and take over when the moment was right. Yet if this person hadn't told anyone his identity, there was nothing to stop Shawiyya from claiming to be the author of this voice once he had the corpse's neck tight between his hands.

Possibly in only a few short days or weeks, he could be wielding more power than he'd ever dreamed possible. The thought warmed him, and he stoked it to almost fever pitch while the laser show overhead continued.

6

Colored pushpins in the wall map marked terrorist attacks across the world. Mack Bolan studied them, saw beyond the coded flags attached to them identifying place and time to focus on the human suffering that stemmed from each casualty.

Barbara Price handed him a cup of steaming coffee. They were in the bedroom that had been assigned to him when he arrived. Brognola and Price had arranged for the wall maps, videos and other information to be ready for his use once he'd checked in.

Despite the burning need inside the big warrior to do something now, he'd heeded Brognola's advice and taken some downtime. As the big Fed had stated, this operation required the mental and physical reserves to manage a precise, surgical strike, not the ability to tilt uselessly at windmills.

Still, Brognola had known Bolan better than to expect him to cool his heels while the rest of the mission's details came trickling in. Less than four hours had passed since Bolan had arrived at the Farm with Grimaldi. He'd spent the time researching the data and making notes in his war book and map case.

There was no question in his mind that he'd be operating in the Middle East.

"Time to take a breather," Price said. She gave him a smile and walked back to the service cart she'd wheeled into the room when she entered. "I took the liberty of raiding the kitchen downstairs before I came up."

Bolan's stomach growled. He'd slept off and on during the flight back to the States, but meals had been hit-and-miss while Grimaldi stopped at military bases long enough to swap for planes that had been ordered into standby. The journey had been like a nightmare pony express ride. By the time they'd touched down at the landing strip at Stony Man, Bolan had had to admit that he was feeling a touch claustrophobic.

Price uncovered the plates. Both held a pair of roast Cornish hens, side dishes of wild rice with almonds, mushrooms and artichokes with lemon butter. A wicker serving bowl in the middle of the table held hot crescent rolls. Dessert was two demitasse cups of whipped cream over chocolate.

They ate in silence. Bolan didn't feel the need to make apologies for the lack of conversation. Price knew him, the drives that motivated him.

She was pouring fresh coffee from the service on the table when the knock sounded on the door.

"Come in," Bolan called.

An armed aide in Stony Man black entered the room with pushpins and a stack of folders. He stopped in front of the wall map and made the insertions quickly.

"Mr. Kurtzman said to tell you they're getting the videos cropped now for the ones we have visuals on."

Bolan nodded his thanks, and the man left the room. Getting up from the chair, he sifted through the half-dozen folders, dropped them one at a time to the desk under the wall map. "Lexington, Kentucky—Transylvania University auditorium was firebombed during a seminar, leaving nine dead and twenty-three hospitalized. London, England—two terrorists were caught trying to place a bomb aboard a British flight to New York. Four policemen were killed and three were injured before the terrorists were subdued by a contingent of SAS. Sacramento, California—terrorists attacked a demonstration by people opposing a forceful reentry into Iraq. Eleven people were killed, forty-one wounded. Bahia Mar, Florida—mortar fire destroyed the offices of the *Chronicle*. Two people were killed, six more hospitalized. Riyadh, Saudia Arabia—at least three teams of terrorists using jeep-mounted TOW missiles took out three oil refineries before being neutralized themselves. They're still sorting through the casualties there. New Orleans, Louisiana—an ROTC group in the field on weekend maneuvers was executed down to the last man. Seventeen dead, including the two instructors."

Price left the service cart and went over to him. "I'm upset too, Mack." Her voice was calm as she searched his eyes. "But we've got to keep believing we can put a stop to this. If we lose hope, if we start doubting each other and our abilities, we'll never even make a successful stand against these people.''

"I know." He let out a tense breath and stared at the new pushpins.

"Terrorism is this," Price said. "It's raw and it's violent, and it's war on innocents. We can't protect them all and you know that. We save those we can, and we grieve for those we can't. There's no other way to fight this.''

"I know. But knowing doesn't help. I want to be out there, doing something."

"Soon. When the time's right." She put her hands on either side of his face and kissed him.

Her lips felt soft, tender. Bolan wrapped his arms around her waist and pulled her close. Her mouth opened under his, and he kissed her deeply.

They were friends, he knew, and nothing more. There was no future for them as anything more than transient lovers. They'd shared laughter and sorrow through missions instigated at Stony Man Farm, won great battles and lost others. But they'd never lost sight of the reasons for the war.

Bolan knew her words were true. A call to action burned within him, filled him with a strong need. But fear was in there, too. Revenge had been the seed that had started the Executioner's one-man war, but hope had tempered it into a grim resolve to fight for what might be, rather than what had been lost.

He gave himself over to the passion that dulled the edge of restlessness stirring inside him. His hands loosened their clothing. She helped him. In moments there was nothing but the feel of skin against skin.

With a quick movement he swept her from her feet and cradled her hard against his chest as he carried her to the bed. He laid her gently in the middle and covered her body with his. Her needs were as strong as his own. He wanted to be tender, but the fear inside them made the pace almost frantic.

Her legs parted and he entered her, thrusting hard while she strained back against him. Her breath was ragged in his ear as she urged him on.

Too soon it was over, both of them shaken and sweat-soaked.

He held her to him, trying to forget for the moment the seriousness of the situation they faced.

SENATOR FRANK KILKENNY got the shakes when he saw the exit signs for the Theodore Roosevelt Bridge. He put both hands on the wheel of his rental car in an attempt to keep them from getting too bad. It never failed.

Ten years gone, and the memories still came back as jagged-toothed as ever.

He blinked blearily at the oncoming traffic. Their headlights only made the alcohol-induced headache slamming between his temples even worse. He made the turn from the Dulles Access Road via the Dulles Connector to I-66. Once he was on the bridge over the Potomac River proper, the shakes got even worse.

Slipping the metal flask of whiskey from his jacket pocket, he uncapped it and took a sip. The fiery liquid burned all the way down. He replaced the flask in his jacket pocket and took an immediate hit of mint-flavored breath spray.

Headlights pulled in behind him and closed the distance.

For a moment he wondered if it was reporters again. Most of them left him alone, but the supermarket tabloids persisted despite the civil suits his family had filed against them.

He glanced to his left, saw the faded patch job construction workers had done ten years ago after the accident. Memories of Donna's screams bubbled through his mind like carbon dioxide from the bottom of a soft drink. He closed his eyes for a moment, then opened them again.

Moonlight splayed across the river's surface. The headlights in his rearview mirror pressed closer.

Without warning, a vehicle in the westbound lane swerved over in front of him, leaving him with no place to go. Horns blared as other cars skidded and barely made clearance.

Kilkenny's foot smashed down on the brake. The rental car shuddered as it came to a metal-grinding stop along the side of the bridge. The car engine stuttered and died.

The senator raised his head warily. Blood dripped from his nose where he'd slammed it into the steering wheel. He lifted his hand to his face, and his fingers came away bright with crimson. More of it flowed and dripped onto his white shirt.

Anger burned in him and took away the fear.

The van that had cut in front of him revved its engine and backed away amid bansheelike wails of torn metal.

Kilkenny tried the door, found he had to ram his shoulder against it to open it. Metal screeched. When it only opened a few inches, he leaned back to hit it with his shoulder again. "You stupid son of a bitch!" he yelled.

His rental car was hit again. It came from behind this time. Off balance from trying for the door again, his head bounced off the steering wheel.

When he found his voice, it was only a croak of fear. His rearview mirror held nothing but the reflected headlights of the car that had rammed him. A shadow crossed into the periphery of his vision moving fast. Moonlight gleamed on metal.

He got the impression of a slender shape, of an elbow coming toward the driver's-side window. Then the safety glass imploded and fell in like a heavy, jointed spiderweb. The metal became a long-barreled pistol that prodded his left cheek.

"Senator Kilkenny?" a sibilant voice asked.

Hoping the man was unsure of who he was, Kilkenny said, "No. You've got the wrong person. I'm not who you think I am."

A face followed the gun in through the window. It was dark-skinned, dark eyes fired by an inner fury.

The teeth in the broad smile were incredibly white. "No, you are *exactly* who I think you are, Senator Kilkenny. We've researched you very well."

Other shadows moved behind the car now. Metal grated in a whirring buzz. He felt vibrations from the rear axle of the rental.

The man tapped Kilkenny's cheek with the barrel of his pistol. "We know, for instance, of your poor friend's death after you drove through the railing of this bridge ten years ago. That incident ended your advancement in a very promising political career. Very sad."

Kilkenny glanced down both ends of the bridge without moving his face. Traffic in both directions was held at bay by orange safety flares placed by two men from the van. His breath came in heaving gasps that seemed to still his heart. Blood covered his mouth. Warm salt coated his tongue.

It seemed the man disappeared in the blink of an eye.

Kilkenny whispered, "Oh God, oh God," and fumbled for the door again. The metal grating at the rear of his vehicle had stopped. His foot had scarcely touched the concrete before the shrill of spinning tires froze him in place.

The van rocketed from the opposite side of the bridge. Headlights glaring like some demented mythical beast, it bore down on him.

Kilkenny yanked his leg back inside the car and tried to take cover in the passenger seat. The metal flask of whiskey went shooting out of his pocket, slid across the cloth interior and banged hollowly from the floorboard. He covered his head as chunks of safety glass from the windshield rained down across his upper body.

The rental literally bounced from the front of the van, settling uneasily.

Kilkenny glanced up between his fingers. The horizon tilted sickeningly. He noticed the railing along the side of the bridge had disappeared. He scrambled for the passenger door, opened it and peered down at the dark water of the Potomac River. His muscles locked when he heard the scream of tortured rubber again. He sobbed down deep in his throat.

Then the impact of the van's second run spilled Kilkenny and his car over the bridge. He was distinctly aware of falling.

Only feet above the river, the car came to a sudden halt.

Kilkenny didn't. He ripped through the broken front windshield flailing like a rag doll. The cold black water closed around him and sucked him down. Then he gained control for just a moment, thought he might even make it when his head broke the surface of the river.

Metal snapped above him.

He looked up just as the car pulled free of the metal cable holding it to the bridge. The vehicle's bulk slammed into him flatly, carried him down.

It took more than an hour for rescue divers to find his remains.

"WE'RE UP AGAINST a terrorist organization the likes of which have never been gathered before." Hal Brognola said.

Mack Bolan sat at one end of the long table in the War Room at the Farm. Phoenix Force and Cowboy John Kissinger sat on one side, leaving the other for Able Team, Jack Grimaldi, Leo Turrin and Barbara Price. Aaron Kurtzman occupied his usual position at the bank of computer keyboards along one wall.

The mood in the room was dark and ominous. Bolan could feel it. The message that Brognola carried to the people assembled here was already known. And each had already set himself for a rebuttal of same.

They were dressed down, wearing jeans, pullovers and joggers. The only hardware in sight were shoulder rigs and hip holsters holding the small arms all were required to carry while at the Farm.

"We've faced terrorist networking a number of times," Brognola continued. "We started uncovering links between terrorist groups in the early eighties. The world was surprised then, and—globally—we started to take notice of what was really shaping up out there."

Bolan sipped his coffee. McCarter cracked the top of another Coke. Hal wasn't covering any new ground here. The Stony Man teams had been formed to combat those terrorist groups and their KGB sponsors.

"Ultimately the United States government is a lot to blame for what the world is facing now." Brognola signaled to Kurtzman.

The room's lights dimmed, and rainbow explosions of color covered the four wall-screens around the group. The pixels rearranged themselves and became a head-and-shoulders picture of Saddam Hussein in full military regalia.

"When Iraq began its war against Iran," Brognola said, "unofficial Intelligence orders were to turn a blind eye to Saddam Hussein and his terrorist connections. In 1982 Iraq was taken off the list of terrorist-supporting nations. With information we've since acquired from the State Department and the CIA, we've confirmed that wasn't the case at all."

A montage of pictures paraded across the screens. Bolan watched in silence. Most of the faces and a number of the incidents were known to him.

Brognola went on. "Hussein came to power in 1979 and pushed the Ba'ath Party into its present position of control. During that time he set up liaisons with the East German Stasi, the Japanese Red Army, the Red Army Faction, the Italian Red Brigades, the Baader-Meinhof and the Irish Republican Army to name a few."

A low rumble of anger ran through the men of Phoenix Force. Only Yakov Katzenelenbogen remained silent. Bolan figured the man maintained a number of ties to the Israeli Mossad that hadn't left him entirely out in the cold concerning Intelligence matters over the intervening years. The Executioner knew Phoenix had fought those terrorists on a number of battlefields despite the State Department's official view of things going on in Iraq.

"Iraq, for a while," Brognola went on, "was *the* place to go for falsified passports for terrorists. It was also a training ground for terrorists. In 1988, when the Eastern Block began to come apart at the seams under economic pressures, Iraq found it necessary to bring new blood into its terrorist armies. It reached out for the Palestine groups and came up with these men."

More pictures scrolled in photographic waves across the screens. Saddam Hussein circulated within a group of men in the same expensive hotel suite surroundings. The Iraqi ex-president seemed jovial and confident as he shook hands and talked with the group of men. From the cut of the photographs, Bolan guessed that very few—perhaps only three or four—had actually been shot at the gathering. The rest had been cut out and blown up from the larger pictures.

"Hussein had them all here," Brognola continued. "Salim Abu Salem, representing the Popular Front for the Liberation of Palestine, Special Command. Nafaf Hawatmeh, representing the Democratic Front for the Liberation of Palestine. Abu Abbas, representing the Palestine Liberation Front. Samir Gousha, representing the Popular Struggle Group. George Habash, representing the Popular Front for the Liberation of Palestine. Abu Ibrahim, representing—in a sense—all of the above because his teachings fathered so many of the terrorist groups. There were others there on the behalf of the May 15 Organization, the Fatah and the Lebanese Armed Revolutionary Faction.''

"True freedom fighters, one and all," David McCarter said sarcastically.

Manning flashed an evil grin. "Sounds like a bomb in the right place could have accomplished miracles that day."

There were nods and voiced agreements around the table.

"The problem with that," Bolan said, "is that kind of move would have left those terrorist organizations with plenty of martyrs to carry on in the memory of."

"Pile up enough martyrs," Carl Lyons said, "and pretty soon there won't be much of a problem left."

Brognola held up his hands for attention. "Sad to say, we didn't have an option on this play. The CIA had a mole deep in the ranks to acquire this, but there was no lead time to develop any kind of scenario. We're dealing with the fruits of those talks now. Khalid Shawiyya has picked up the reins where Saddam left off."

"There is also a rumor of someone who is overseeing the newly developed terrorist network," Katz said.

Heads swiveled in his direction.

When Kurtzman turned around from his keyboard arrangement, Bolan knew the information Katz had was new to Stony Man's cybernetic systems, as well.

"I have no names." The Phoenix Force team leader opened his hand palm-up. "Only rumors have surfaced so far. My contacts within the Mossad have been grudging at best since I've been with Phoenix and with Stony Man. They don't know what it is I do, are unsure sometimes of exactly what I fight for if I'm not solely for Israel. But I have friends left. Just before this meeting I received an answer to a discreet inquiry I launched a few hours ago.''

"The Mossad knew about Hussein's meeting?" Bolan asked.

"Yes. They imparted the knowledge to the CIA through channels that couldn't be traced back to them."

Brognola nodded, letting everyone in the room know the information jibed with what he'd gotten.

"The Mossad is convinced this unknown man is not only running the terrorist network, but can also pull considerable weight in most of the Middle Eastern countries unfriendly to America. There might even be enough of a push involved to get countries who straddle the line, like Syria, to despose the present government and realign those countries with Iraq."

"The Mossad sees Shawiyya as the ringleader in this?" Jack Grimaldi asked.

"No. The man has more sheer animal cunning than political savvy. Iraq is only the figurehead for the movement."

"But it's shaping up to be one hell of a movement," Calvin James said.

"What about Arafat?" Leo Turrin asked. "Seems like he and the PLO are kind of missing from the picture."

"Not anymore," Barbara Price replied. "From the Intel we've received, the PLO is deeply entrenched in this thing whether Arafat is or not."

"There aren't any guesses as to who this mystery man might be?" Rosario Blancanales asked.

"No," Katz said.

Brognola shook his head. "We've had a glimmer of him. That's all." He turned back to the screen and extended a metal pointer toward the display monitor in front of him.

The keys of Kurtzman's computer clacked, and the four screens changed. Maps of the world spread across the walls. The shadows of Brognola's pointer touched them all.

"There's no doubt of Iraq's place as the hotbed of the terrorist activity," Brognola said. The pointer rested on Baghdad. "But thinking in the Intelligence circles is that Shawiyya is just a puppet having his strings pulled. Our mission is to find out the truth and negate the opposition. They're operating, as you know, in domestic theaters, as well as internationally."

Price stood. "Able Team will be responsible for terrorist attacks in the United States. From the indications we've seen, there has to be a terrorist command post operating within our borders. The attacks have been too systematic, too punctual to believe anything else. Whether they're operating independently, following a series of directions or taking orders straight from Baghdad, we need to find them and take them down. We'll be working out of several offices while we pursue them, but the overall umbrella will be Justice Department Sensitive Operations Group. We'll have a blank check in most areas, coming straight out of the President's office."

"Won't cut much ice when it comes to jurisdictional disputes," Lyons said. "Police departments are touchy about little things like that."

"We'll smooth them over as best we can," Price told him. "If we can't operate with these people, we'll operate without them."

"Fair enough," Schwarz said.

"Your first objective is in New York City," Price said. "According to Intel that Aaron has gleaned from his sources, a major passport scam has been set up in Brooklyn to get the terrorists into this country. You'll have to find it, shut it down and get as much information as you can about the people already processed."

"Whatever records you can gather up," Kurtzman said, "can be forwarded to the Farm. I've got a team standing by to start interpreting and disseminating it as needed."

Lyons nodded.

"Striker," Brognola said.

The walls melted, went back to a much more detailed map of Iraq and Kuwait.

"I'm sure you knew where you were headed." Brognola tapped Kuwait City with the pointer. "Colonel Rance Pollock has officially been reinstated to his post in the Army. Orders have already been cut for you to take command of a field garrison in Kuwait City. Your second-in-command is Lieutenant Colonel Joshua Eldridge. Whatever missions you see fit to undertake will be backed by General Lincoln Armstrong and his support teams."

The walls shrunk in on themselves, then exploded with renewed color. A series of photos followed, all centering around a big man in Army dress. In most of them the man was a major. He was big and blocky and looked as if he'd been put together out of railroad ties and shaped with a wood chisel. His china blue eyes held an innocence his scarred hands and lined face denied. A desert tan marred his complexion, but he wore the uniform with obvious pride. And there was something else that went with the uniform and the position. Bolan noticed it after only a few photographs. Eldridge kept a firm distance between himself and his men. It was evident even in the pictures of ground warfare staged in the last war with Iraq.

"Eldridge just made lieutenant colonel a few months ago," Brognola said. "He distinguished himself in service during the ground war in Kuwait and southern Iraq. He's in his early forties and has been a career soldier since eighteen. The feeling in the Pentagon is that Eldridge is just the man to help coordinate behind-the-lines search-and-destroy missions against Khalid Shawiyya and his war machine. And that's what the President wants you to do, Striker— take this operation just as deeply into the heart of that bastard Shawiyya's house as you can.''

7

Mack Bolan watched the series of photographs of Lieutenant Colonel Joshua Eldridge fade from the screen as he refilled his cup from the coffeepot beside the wall. He gazed over the men assembled in the room. Most of them, in one way or another, were there because of him. He'd broken a bloody path for justice that hadn't been dared before, and set into motion a violent chain of events that could swallow them all.

When Stony Man Farm had first been designed, its goals were surgical strikes that were to be neither retaliatory nor anticipatory. They were to remove hostile aggressors before the big plays had time to take place.

Now it seemed the brave few in this room were arrayed against the whole terrorist might of the Middle East. The forces they faced were a rolling juggernaut of death and destruction seasoned by decades of modern warfare.

And he knew there wasn't a person in the room who would back down from the challenge.

Brognola addressed the men of Phoenix Force. "Your target is going to be the unrest surrounding Israel. Our Intel also indicates another large terrorist cell gathered on the West Bank readying a strike that will shake the Israelis from their defensive posture faster than a swarm of mad hornets leaving the nest. Tel Aviv is on the brink of declaring martial law and taking command of the area by force. I'm sure you're all aware of the problems they've been facing there."

"What's our specific objective?" Katzenelenbogen asked.

"Find the terrorist cell," Brognola said. "Then cut off the head and disperse the information you're able to retrieve to the Mossad. If we can do this, they've agreed to work in the shadows and stay out of a heads-up confrontation with Shawiyya and Iraq."

"The State people must have made some heavy-duty promises to get the Israeli government to fall in line behind them like that," Rafael Encizo said.

"The Man made the promises," Brognola replied, "and he was banking on us when he did."

Silence fell over the room for a moment.

"Got something hot coming in," Kurtzman announced. He wheeled to address the monitor and keyboard. "Going on-screen with it now."

Video footage, reproduced through computer-generated images, scanned across the four walls.

Bolan watched with interest. He recognized the Theodore Roosevelt Bridge easily.

On-screen a winch truck on one bank reeled in a cable connected to a smashed car. Ripples played out across the river from the twisted metal. Divers in police uniforms and scuba gear surfaced out in the river occasionally like feeding goldfish. A man with clean-cut features and styled hair that didn't blow in the wind suddenly took up half the available view. He held a microphone in one hand and spoke, but the audio was cut out of the reception.

"What are we looking at?" Barbara Price asked.

"News footage from a local station," Kurtzman answered. He held a pair of headphones to one ear. "According to the reporter, that car was a rental from Dulles. It was leased to Frank Kilkenny."

"The senator from Pennsylvania?" Lyons asked.

"Yeah," Kurtzman said. "One-time favorite son candidate for the presidency." His fingers blurred across the keyboard.

"What about Kilkenny?" Bolan asked. He figured he already knew the answer, but hearing it would take away the wondering that left a cold knot in his stomach.

"Dead," Kurtzman replied. "The police diving team has already recovered his body. They're searching the river now for any other passengers."

"How did he go off the bridge?" Schwarz asked.

"He was forced off by two vehicles driven by dark-skinned men. Must have been a good dozen people there when it went down."

The screens shifted focus. Pixels changed colors as skillfully as a chameleon. When the view was resolved, Bolan scanned the landscape, realized they were seeing it from a helicopter.

The camera and chopper moved in, trailed a smoking wreath that curled from a large house flanked by a barn and a series of corrals. Orange tongues of fire still lapped at the wreckage of the house.

"This is outside Modesto, California," Kurtzman said. "You're looking at the home of Lyle Crane."

"The congressman?" Calvin James asked.

Kurtzman nodded. "Also predicted to go far politically."

Price picked up the phone beside her place at the table. She got up as she dialed, then walked to a corner of the room for privacy.

"The election this year is going to leave a lot of people out in the open," Lyons said. "Candidates are going to be like sitting ducks. Every camera they reach out for to get publicity or converts to their camp could have a sniper scope attached to it."

The thought hung heavily in the room.

Bolan sipped his coffee and chased the nightmare through his mind. "The candidates are running a high profile with it being an election year anyway. Assassinations of those people will guarantee even more news coverage and make it harder to maintain security."

Price returned and put down the phone. "The Secret Service is already aware of the situation. But they're way understaffed to handle anything of this scale."

"Which means local PDs are going to be swamped trying to contain it." Lyons sat back in his chair with a sour look on his face. "With this much political pressure rolling down and the kind of overtime we're talking about here for the average joe cop, states with favorite-son candidates or real competitors for the office are going to be ripe for a lot of trigger-happy mistakes. If this situation goes on very long, you're going to see cops start shooting at shadows. Not to mention the fact that it takes them out of an investigatory mode and throws them into a purely reactionary stance. The streets in those cities are going to go deaf, dumb and blind."

A tight frown fitted itself to Brognola's face. The big Fed pulled a cigar from his jacket, unwrapped it and locked it between his teeth.

Abruptly the wall screens cleared and new images formed.

The current series of shots came from inside a large government building where a passionate speech was in progress.

The speaker was lean and dark, dressed in a conservative business suit with a *ghutra* covering his head. The nose was large, the most prominent feature on a handsome face. The mustache beneath was only now beginning to color with gray. The man shouted as he spoke to the crowd of Arabic people standing and clapping before him. Uniformed security guards hung back with their AK-47s across their chests. He wrapped a hand into a fist and shook it at the sky. Most of the crowd followed suit.

"Damascus, Syria," Kurtzman said in clipped tones. "We're running on a one-minute delayed reception." He held a hand to the ear phone covering one ear and watched the screens with the other Stony Man people. He was obviously counting the time off against the clock flicking through numbers on the monitor in front of him. "You're watching Hamoud Jaluwi delivering a speech to the section of the Syrian Ba'athist Party sympathetic to Iraq's position against the United States. He's urging war." The big cybernetics expert was obviously listening to an interpretation of the speech. "He's asking for Syrians with the future of the Arab world in mind to link forces with Shawiyya and Iraq against the Western world."

"He'll have people listening to him," McCarter said grimly. "That man runs the underground movement in Syria, and they've bloody well almost overtaken al-Assad's efforts at ruling the country."

Jaluwi continued to shout and wave his fist.

"Now," Kurtzman said. His fingers played across the keyboard. Events changed into a slow rush on the wall screens.

"Sniper," Blancanales said. "In the corner at two o'clock."

Bolan had already noted the gunman. The figure was indistinct on the balcony overlooking the amphitheater. The matte black finish of the rifle barrel absorbed the light, but became highly visible when he tuned his eye to take in what *wasn't* there.

A muzzle-flash licked out, spread like molasses under the slo-mo effect generated by the computer.

Hamoud Jaluwi tumbled backward a heartbeat later, his arms and legs flailing as he was yanked from the ground by the impact that struck his forehead.

The computer dumped everything back into real time when Kurtzman punched in another series of commands. There was an abrupt time change.

"There's no delay now," Kurtzman said. "You're seeing actual footage as it happens."

Bolan leaned forward. The crowd surged, turned around and sank in on itself. A human ladder seemed to form out of bodies and rise up toward the second-story balcony. The camera blurred out of focus for a moment, then centered in on a zoom lens. Three uniformed security guards heaved a man over the balcony railing toward the crowd. They swept the man away like a mongrel hoard ravening for dinner.

A computer-generated window opened up on the wall screens. In it, the assassin's face was frozen at a thirty-degree angle. The crowd continued to assault the sniper—clothing tore, flesh was shredded shortly afterward. Blood smeared some of the angry and frightened faces.

In the computer window the sniper's face righted. It was lean, sallow, definitely European. Fine blond hair was matted to the man's scalp. His brown eyes were wide with fear.

Abruptly the picture blinked and changed. It was the same man, but in this pose he looked somber. His eyes were hooded. The picture split within the window, became front and right profiles. Computer lettering jotted into place below the window as the Syrian mob raged on and continued tearing bloody pieces from the corpse. The uniformed security people waded into the middle of the crowd using their rifle butts. They were repulsed by the throng of avengers in seconds.

"Grant Connor," Kurtzman said while reading the information that flowed across his computer monitor. "He was CIA and known in Intelligence circles as a take-out artist. Currently he was one of ours, but it's been discovered that he'd been doubling for the Israelis."

"Shit," Brognola said in disgust.

KHALID SHAWIYYA COULDN'T keep the smile from his face as he replayed the videotape of Hamoud Jaluwi on the big-screen TV in his private quarters. After the fifth time he switched it off with the remote control, then got up and poured himself a glass of distilled water. Even in his private life he lived out the edicts of his chosen religion. If a man was going to become something, he had to become it. He couldn't merely paint on a face. Alcohol would no longer be found in the presidential palace even for foreign guests.

A part of him felt sorry for Hamoud Jaluwi. The man had served to represent the militant aspect of

Syria that had wanted to throw in with Iraq during the first war with the Americans. Syria's president was an ambitious and harsh man. The politician had taken the stance against Saddam Hussein and Iraq by faulting Saddam for creating enough of a disturbance to draw American military forces into the Middle East in staggering numbers.

Jaluwi had held power, but it hadn't been enough. It wouldn't ever have been enough to pull the country together while the man remained alive. Yet Jaluwi's death might be enough to pull the nation across the line and commit them to Iraq's cause.

It was unbelievably stupid for the Americans or Israelis to make this kind of mistake and give the Arab world their first martyr.

But he didn't intend to let the opportunity pass him by.

He crossed the room, pressed the buzzer on his hand-carved desk and summoned his secretary. It was time for another news conference, and he intended to make Jaluwi very much a part of it, embroider the events with righteous indignation. There'd be new converts for a violent retribution against the United States by nightfall. The terrorist network operating out of his country could swell.

And maybe his championing of the avenging force stemming from Jaluwi's death would be enough to make his fellow Arab leaders look at him in a new light. Once he managed to find and silence the mysterious voice that whispered threats and orders over the phone, maybe they would turn to him for the guidance they needed to achieve their ends.

They also serve who are dead and gone. He smiled at the thought. Then he toasted Jaluwi's memory with his dark reflection in the blank television screen.

"I'VE GOT A MESSAGE coming in from the White House," Kurtzman said.

Mack Bolan marked the time automatically. Thirteen minutes had passed since the bloody execution of CIA agent Grant Connor. The news reception from Damascus had ended abruptly seven minutes ago when uniformed guards swarmed over the news people and confiscated cameras and tape recorders.

The President's face filled all four screens. The Man looked grave and worried, his face ashen and his eyes washed out behind his glasses.

A videocamera above the wall screen to the left of the table in the War Room hummed as it focused on the group. The Executioner knew the visual and auditory communications went both ways via a special satellite arrangement with attached scrambler.

"Hal."

"Here, Mr. President." Brognola turned to face the camera above the wall screen. It hummed and whirred as it locked in on the big Fed.

"I've just talked to the director of the CIA." The President laced his fingers on the desk before him. "I've been assured we had nothing to do with the assassination that just took place in Syria."

"We have information that Connor was one of theirs," Brognola said.

"Yes. So I've been told. I was also informed that the agent was also working with the Mossad. He'd been under investigation for the past two months. Connor had been thought responsible for compromising at least three highly sensitive missions involving the Palestinian issue."

"Perhaps Connor was working under their orders," Brognola suggested.

The President shook his head. "I talked to the Israeli prime minister only a few moments ago. I was assured that wasn't the case."

"Their Intelligence agencies have the same problems as ours, sir," Brognola responded. "It could be a case of one hand not knowing what the other was doing."

"Granted, but for the moment I'm willing to believe what they tell me. If you or your people find out anything differently, we'll go to cases then." The President cleared his throat. "The CIA director also told me that Connor wasn't even assigned to Syria. His post had been in the Baltic countries. Three weeks ago he disappeared. Until today there'd been a very quiet manhunt going on over in Lithuania."

"The CIA had no idea Connor was in Syria?" Bolan asked.

The camera, controlled from one of the boards within Kurtzman's reach, rolled around on its mounts and came to a stop facing the warrior.

"None at all, Striker," the President replied.

"The man had to have left tracks," Bolan said. "It might be an idea if the CIA concentrated on how Connor was able to achieve entrance into the country. If he didn't have the proper papers and credentials to move freely in that area, he must have used people they're familiar with to get them."

"Care to share your reasoning behind this request?"

"It could be a suck play," Bolan replied. "Suppose Connor was set up by the terrorist network to take the fall for Jaluwi's death? A lot of public resentment is going to follow the assassination once the news services release Connor's identity. It could have been used to generate those feelings."

The President picked up a pencil and made a brief note on a pad outside the camera's view. "Point taken. I'll get people on it immediately. If your assumption proves true, we can expose this for the sham it is and perhaps deflect some of the animosity that'll be coming from those countries." He looked back into the camera. "Gentlemen, and Miss Price, I know you'll soon be involved in struggles of your own concerning the violence that surrounds us. I want you to know that I'm standing by each and every one of you. If there is anything I can do, let me know. Good luck, and God keep."

The wall screens blanked.

The warriors around the table stirred restlessly. Bolan finished his coffee, feeling the same urge to do something that fired the others.

Barbara Price stood. "There's one other thing to add, Striker." She nodded at Kurtzman.

The big man's fingers caressed the keyboard.

The screens glimmered.

"As Colonel Rance Pollock, you'll have the U.S. Army running maneuvers as you see fit while in Kuwait and—in all probability—Iraq. Hal and I have added another layer of offensive weaponry to your collection." A slight smile twisted Price's lips. "A surprise package, you might say."

The screens cleared, revealing the face of a tawny-haired woman with light hazel eyes and skin tanned the color of supple doeskin leather. The picture changed. The woman stood surprisingly tall against a black-suited Middle Eastern diplomat at an international ballroom gathering. She wore a party dress of shimmering silver with a plunging neckline that revealed a lot of healthy flesh. Her smile was white, beautiful, but her eyes showed none of her mirth. A neutral sheen flattened them and made them distant. Bolan was sure the man she was with hadn't been aware of her eyes at all. She wore gloves as she held her drink. Bolan guessed it was more to prevent her fingerprints from being taken than an attempt at sophisticated chic.

Price glanced at Bolan. "Do you know her?"

"No."

"How about the name Talia Alireza?"

The Executioner leaned back in his seat and studied the woman in the silver dress in a new light. "Mercenary. Works primarily in Europe and Asia, but the Intel I have on her suggests that she's of Middle Eastern origin. Pictures of her are said not to exist, but she works steady and pulls down top dollar in the protection-and-surveillance side of things."

"She's ex-Mossad," Katzenelenbogen stated.

"We didn't turn that up in our search," Price said.

Katz waved his hand. "Nor will you. She was very deep inside the infrastructure ten years ago. She was merely a girl, barely past college age. Things happened. She decided to leave. Her file was buried along with other files."

"Alireza isn't your typical Jewish name," Blancanales observed.

"She's half-Jewish," Price said, "and half Iraqi."

"Must have made for a tough childhood," James said.

"That's only the tip of the iceberg." Price gazed up at the face on the screens. She folded her arms across her breasts. "Her father was an Israeli mole stationed in Iraq. He was assigned to watch Brigadier Abd al-Karim al-Qasim's rise to power after the Free Officers' ouster of the British in 1958. While he was there he met and married an Iraqi woman and fathered Talia. In the early seventies, when Saddam Hussein and the Ba'athist party were assuming total control of the country, her father was discovered to be a spy. An

Israeli Mossad force intercepted the Iraqi Intelligence team before interrogation measures could begin. After that, things get hazy.''

"The Alireza family," Katz continued in a slow voice, "were transferred back to Tel Aviv. Their surnames were dropped and the father's name was used once more.''

"You have more than we do," Price said.

The Phoenix Force leader nodded. "This is very confidential material I'm giving you. I was aware of the situation while it was going on.''

"What can you tell us?''

"Talia was a child when she was brought to Tel Aviv. She was immediately surrounded by a culture she and her mother were raised to hate and think of as enemies. Neither fit in. They had only each other. Her father returned to work for the Mossad. His relationship with Talia's mother was only for the cover she provided. He treated Talia more as a possession than his flesh and blood. Still, though, she loved him as a child will love its father no matter what wrong is done.''

"I'd heard her mother was dead," Price said.

"I can't say. Less than two years after her arrival in Israel, Talia's mother disappeared. Perhaps she's dead by now.''

"And Talia?" Leo Turrin asked.

"Left with her father.''

"Her mother never gave her a choice about going?" Turrin asked.

"No."

A grim frown twisted the stocky little Fed's face. "Little girl lost," he said in a soft voice.

Bolan saw the pain flash in his friend's eyes. As head over prostitution in the Mafia's flesh-eating chain for a number of years, Leo "the Pussy" Turrin had seen a lot of little girls lost. And he remembered every damn one of them he hadn't been able to save, including the Executioner's own sister.

"She was." Katz picked up his narrative. "Once deserted by her mother, she had nowhere to turn but to her father. Only he was never there. The Mossad during those days was very busy. There'd been the Munich murders, as you recall, and infiltration in Iraq to destroy the nuclear reactor near Baghdad in 1981. When she came of age, Talia applied for military training and moved into the Mossad. She proved a very capable operative."

"But she left the Mossad," Price said.

"She was betrayed," Katz replied. "A superior set her up to be killed. He'd never approved of her being in the Mossad. He was convinced the twelve years she'd spent in Baghdad had scarred her thinking for life. He wanted to take no chances that she would defect with all the knowledge she had of Mossad operations. She was better trained than her superior believed her to be, and she escaped with her life. It wasn't until years later the Mossad discovered she'd reentered espionage circles under her old name. During that time her father had been killed, and the superior suffered an accident that left him on a life-support system for nine years before he died."

"She's never operated within the Middle East since her break with the Mossad," Kurtzman said. "But she's clearly maintained her sources. She pushed new information our way since coming on board these past few hours."

"She approached the United States about joining the effort against Iraq?" Bolan asked.

Price nodded. "I've talked to her. Talia's reasoning is that if something isn't done to quell the threat of Shawiyya and the terrorist networks, there's going to be a big radioactive crater where the Middle East used to be. She doesn't want that to happen. It doesn't have anything to do with nationality, according to her. She feels the innocents that remain in that sphere of influence need to be protected. The best way to do that, she says, is to end hostilities as quickly as possible." Stony Man's mission controller shifted her gaze to Bolan. "The call belongs to you about whether to leave her in or out. You're at ground zero there. But if you're as convinced of her intentions as I am, I think she and her team could prove valuable. Not everything you choose to do can be accomplished by American military men. Especially when you're operating behind the lines. She knows the country, and she knows the players."

"Set up a meet," Bolan said. "We'll see how things shape up." He stared at the face of Talia Alireza with renewed interest.

Brognola cued Kurtzman, and the lights came back on. His face was grim as he surveyed the Stony Man warriors. "I don't need to emphasize the need for successes here. Every minute we waste could ultimately mean the sacrifice of a dozen innocents. Here *and* there. We're at war, and we're—" he glanced at a piece of paper on the table in front of him "—two thousand thirteen lives down as of now. Catching up isn't the option we're after here. We've been called in to prevent things from becoming worse. Any way we can. We've been offered no quarter, and I'll be damned if we give one."

8

The Bahrainian airport was crowded and busy. Talia
Alireza watched the groups of men, women and children around her with a careful eye. Her personal radar tingled in warning. She hadn't seen anyone who
promised a threat to her, but she knew that person or
persons were there.

She waited apart from everyone as the mechanized
luggage belts ferried trunks and suitcases around in a
circle. She let her luggage pass three times as the waiting crowd thinned. It was too easy to step forward
within the clutch of bodies and plunge an icepick or
dagger through the heart. She knew because she'd
done it herself upon occasion.

Normally the carryon would have been in her possession when she left the plane. However, these weren't
normal times. The airport authorities had taken all
luggage away to be stored and searched. Her flight had
been delayed for hours by the extra security precau-
tions.

She gripped the carryon in her right hand. A waiting assassin might not think her as quick to react with
her left hand. She'd trained hard to neutralize her

right-handedness. Now she was almost ambidextrous.

Heads turned her way as intrigued males gazed at her with sometimes open speculation. Part of it, she knew, was her height. A six-foot-tall woman in this part of the world was unusual. During European and American contracts, she'd often been able to disguise it by wearing flats when the other women in the group wore heels. And sometimes she operated so far behind the scenes that no one ever saw her anyway.

She wore faded blue jeans with tears at the knees and one denim pocket ripped away over her hip. A loose purple blouse, buttoned high enough to hint at the promised cleavage beneath, was tucked into her waistband. A wide belt with a carved wooden buckle filled the loops. Her sunglasses were so dark her eyes couldn't be seen. She'd left her tawny-colored hair loose, and it brushed against her shoulders. She carried no purse and wore no makeup.

With the carryon over her shoulder she walked toward the airport entrance through the milling crowds. A man fell into her wake like a shark trailing chum bait.

Talia kept her pace to a normal walk and altered her course without seeming to do so. She studied her tail in the glass wall separating the gift shop from the normal flow of passenger traffic.

He was tall, with thick Slavic features. His suit was cheap, dark but not quite black, and had an Eastern cut. He carried his hat in his hand, fingers tucked securely in the brim. His image disappeared as the glass wall played out.

Talia felt a fresh supply of adrenaline churn into her system. She kept it stoked and in reserve, waited for the proper moment to unleash it.

She passed through the door to the women's room, her hands already busy. Only two other stalls were occupied. She chose the one next to the last one. Inside, she hung her carryon from the hook mounted on the door. The carved belt buckle came loose instantly, separating from the leather and leaving the belt itself intact around her waist. It felt compact and solid in her clenched fist.

Her other hand freed three triangular blades from the underwiring in her bra. They slid into the wooden buckle and locked into place between her splayed fingers. Four inches of dark, sharp steel protruded from each blade.

She pushed her breath out easily, let it refill her lungs automatically without forcing it. Her mind focused. The adrenaline edge swirled within her as it waited to be released.

The women in the other stalls left.

No one else entered.

Then tentative footsteps shuffled across the tiled floor.

Talia waited in the enclosure. Her hand was a bone-and-muscle knot around the spiked belt buckle. She resisted the impulse to peer over the top of the wall.

Her pursuer began opening stalls.

Heartbeats hammered by. She smelled his after-shave, laced heavily with sweat and the boredom of waiting. Spicy food had fogged his breath.

Something with a metallic surface grazed the door of her cubicle. When the door exploded inward, she caught a glimpse of the big man's face, then the fingers of her free hand curled around the enameled metal panel. She added force to the door's own rebound from the wall.

The man's silenced automatic came up as he went for a two-handed grip. The door, with her weight behind it, slammed into his elbow. Two silenced shots whispered by her, gouging long scars from the metal walls and tearing ceramic scabs from the wall behind her. A third shot exploded the porcelain bowl of the commode. Hissing like a serpent, water rushed from the fragments of the toilet and covered the floor.

Concentrating on the feel of the weapon in her hand, Talia raked the sharp claws across the man's throat. Warmth splashed over her fingers. There was only a moment of tangible flesh that she felt, then the blades slid through.

Three more shots tore into the acoustic tiles of the ceiling as the man fell backward. Blood covered the front of his chest like a gruesome bib. Propelled by wheezing breaths that no longer went through the proper channels, crimson bubbles raced down his neck.

Before the man's movement on the tiled floor had a chance to come to a complete stop, Talia was in motion. She leaped foward, her hand bristling with claws drawn back for another blow if it was needed.

It wasn't. The edges of the wounds were maggot white from loss of blood. Already the pumping spurts from the severed carotid had died away to thick, sluggish trickles.

The man tried to raise the pistol, and Talia kicked it from his hand.

The light dimmed in his eyes and went away.

Hypnotized as always by the sight of death descending on a victim, whether by her hand or another's, she turned her attention to the rest of her situation. A glance at the door showed the slim metal band that jammed the lock.

Knowing she had time, she knelt quickly and went through the man's pockets. The cigarettes were Russian, meaning he'd only just arrived in the past day or so. Customs didn't allow much imported tobacco, and the nicotine stains on his fingers told of a serious habit that would have consumed the allowable amount very quickly.

Water continued to pool around her from the broken toilet, trace elements of clotting blood running through it like tiny islands. Chill crept up along her thighs from her drenched knees resting against the tiled floor.

A keyring to a rental car was in another pocket, along with a small collection of Bahrainian coins. An indentation on his left ring finger spoke of usual jewelry that had been left behind. The watch was cheap.

Two more clips for the Norinco Type 59 Makarov were in an inside jacket pocket.

The papers in his wallet were undoubtedly false. They identified the man as an Australian, and Talia was sure he'd never been there. But they had a familiar look to them that might provide a clue as to his definite identity. She guessed Soviet, perhaps KGB, but didn't see the connection.

A tentative knock sounded on the door, followed by an inquiring voice.

Gritting her teeth with effort, she managed to get the loose corpse up from the floor and into the stall next to the one with the broken toilet. It wasn't a clever hiding place, but it might buy her some time. The running water spattered underfoot. To further confuse things, she tugged the man's pants down around his ankles.

Then she locked the door from the inside and scrambled over the top of the stall.

Glancing briefly into a mirror above one of the sinks, she washed the blood spatters from her face, pulled her hair back to conceal the clots that had landed there and shrugged out of the purple blouse.

The door rattled as someone tried the handle. A couple of voices spoke outside it now.

She threw the purple blouse in the trashcan, added the razor claw. There was nothing in it that could be tied to her. She pulled on a loose-fitting beige blouse from her carryon that would draw attention to her breasts and not her abdomen. She changed magazines in the silenced pistol, inserting a full clip. It only took a few strips from the roll of surgical tape she habitually carried in her personal things to secure the Makarov to the smooth flesh of her stomach. The resulting bulge was camouflaged by the loose shirt. She taped the spare clip to the back of one of her calves under the jeans.

With her sunglasses back in place, she went to the door, opened it and followed the inch-deep water out into the airport hallway. The half-dozen women dodged back from the small wave quickly, cursing in different languages.

"There's a repairman inside," Talia said in English. "He's working on the facilities and will have them back in order as soon as possible." She excused herself and headed for the entrance again. She kept her left arm in close to help support the Makarov.

The women kept talking and backing away from the swirling water.

Bright sunlight filled the city as Talia pushed through the double doors. The air was hot and dry, making her more aware of the sticky fluid in her hair.

"Cab, miss?"

She turned at the sound of the familiar voice speaking Arabic.

Cast in dark ebony, with a smooth-shaved head and clad in a white shirt, boots and khaki pants, Jimoh touched the brim of his cap and opened the door of his taxi. His dark eyes touched hers only briefly, then continued to sweep the surrounding area as much as possible without making his observations noticeable.

As she slid into the rear seat, she reached under the loose blouse and freed the Makarov. Placing it under her right thigh, she watched the airport crowd while Jimoh squeezed his blocky frame under the steering column.

"Trouble?" he asked as he slipped the transmission into gear.

"One man inside," she said.

"Israeli?"

"No. Russian, I think. We'll do some inquiring."

Jimoh pulled away from the curb and neatly into traffic. He glanced at her in the rearview mirror. "I still think we should reconsider this job. Wars the size this one promises to be are never really good for someone who makes a living as a mercenary. You know that."

She nodded and flipped the latches on the briefcase on the seat beside her. The lid opened easily. Inside was an Uzi submachine gun and six spare 32-round clips in foam cutouts. A sheen of oil covered them, made them glisten and filled the interior of the cab with the odor. Satisfied, she closed the case.

"I know," she said tersely.

"I've never seen you be self-destructive, Talia." His voice was low, honest.

She returned his gaze in the rearview mirror full measure. "I haven't lost any objectivity here. The Americans are paying good money for our services."

"We don't need the money." Jimoh crossed his hands over the steering wheel, made the turn smoothly onto the highway that would take them to the causeway linking Bahrain and Saudi Arabia. Other connections and contacts she had in place there would begin the various stages needed to push her and her forces into Kuwait. "We're more flush now than we've ever been."

"I've always planned for the future in spite of the present," she snapped.

Jimoh regarded her with his dead eyes. "Talia, you set up the rules when we formed this minicorporation. The first one you laid down is that there would be no work done in the Middle East. Now you're breaking that. It makes me curious."

"There's nothing to worry about. It's business as usual."

"Except we're breaking a cardinal rule."

"Jimoh?"

"Yes?"

"Are we being followed?"

Jimoh's eyes tightened slightly. "No, ma'am."

Talia sighed. She positively hated it when he interjected that cool note of indifference in his words. "Look, I apologize. I was out of line."

"Maybe you were."

"You're not making this easy."

He smiled slightly. "No, ma'am."

She settled back in the seat and watched the landscape around them. Ornate and overly large in some instances, the buildings seemed to spring up from the desert flanking them. Only occasionally could the narrow strip of fertile land to the north be seen. "The money *is* good," she said after a moment.

"But we could pass it up."

"Yes."

"And you don't want to."

"I don't know yet."

Minutes later the cool blue of the Gulf of Bahrain slid away to either side of the causeway.

Jimoh looked into the rearview mirror and caught her gaze. "You know," he said softly, "guilt is often a more deadly emotion than even love. With guilt you sometimes think you deserve the hurt and pain that comes your way."

She hesitated. "I know." There was nothing else she could say. Jimoh could see through her well enough to recognize the lies.

"YOUR CALL, IRONMAN."

Carl Lyons looked at the small restaurant through the dirt-smeared windshield of his rental car. Red-and-white-checked curtains covered both ends of the plate-glass window that filled up nearly sixty percent of the available storefront. "Geppetto's" was written in peeling black paint in the upper left-hand corner. A polished brass entrance sign hung beside the only door. The overall color scheme was red and white, and went well with the barbershop's decor next door.

"Let's do it," Lyons said in answer to Blanca-nales's question. He loosened the strap snugging the Colt Government .45 in shoulder leather. He looked at his passenger. "You ready?"

Leo Turrin nodded. "As I'm gonna be." He took a pair of Smith & Wesson Model 649 Bodyguards from ankle holsters and dropped them into the pockets of his trench coat.

Lyons slipped on a pair of aviator sunglasses, and both men got out of the car. Under the trench coat Turrin wore an expensive three-piece suit that he still managed to slouch in. Lyons wore a long black leather dress jacket that hung past his hips and easily covered the shoulder-slung .45 and the Python .357 holstered at his back. Attached to his left wrist was a gambler's hideout rig sporting a Semmerling LM-4 .45 ACP derringer.

Halfway across the street Lyons could feel the eyes of watchers on him. His gut tightened. He folded the tension into a little ball inside his stomach, then breathed it out. He covered Turrin's flank as they made the door.

Inside it was dim. At two in the afternoon there weren't many customers. Lyons figured most of them for Don Fioretti's people. His mind automatically flipped through the mug shots he'd never forget from his years on the LAPD police force. He made two people, both torpedoes with a history of unsubstantiated executions. He wondered if they could still smell the cop scent on him. Some things never washed away.

The service area was in the back. A polished wooden counter looked as if it held up an old Italian man in a cheap suit, and corralled a trio of waitresses. The girls looked young and tired, but a flicker of excitement glowed in their eyes as they saw four big men get up from their table near the door.

Lyons took a step off to the right to get a clear line of fire. He didn't go unnoticed.

"Hey, Don Fioretti," Turrin called out in a light voice, "is this any way to greet an *amico?*" He raised his arms and held them out at his sides.

The four men spread out among the islands of the tables and slowed their approach. They glanced back over their shoulders awaiting further instructions.

Seconds still counting down inside his head, Lyons knew Schwarz and Blancanales would be in position within heartbeats.

Eduardo Fioretti squinted and looked at Turrin with new interest. Dark bags hung under his eyes, and his skin was wrinkled and drained from the passage of years. Only a few strands of hair remained atop his head, and they were carefully oiled down.

"Leo?" Fioretti called out in a raspy voice. "Leo the Pussy?"

Turrin gave the man a cocky grin and lowered his arms. "In the flesh Don Fioretti."

"As you always were," Fioretti said, then laughed. The men around the table joined him obediently.

"Come, come over here, Leo." Fioretti waved to Turrin, who crossed the room.

Lyons started after him.

The four men threading through the tables insinuated themselves between Lyons and the Mafia Don.

"Hang back, Vinnie," Turrin said with a smile. "Let me and Don Fioretti get reacquainted first." He looked at Fioretti. "We're all friends here."

"Yeah, yeah, sure," the old man said.

Lyons stood in place, his arms crossed over his chest. He didn't like being this far out of the action, then thought Schwarz and Blancanales had probably liked it even less.

"Have you eaten?" Fioretti snapped his fingers.

Instantly the old man and the trio of waitresses by the counter started forward.

Turrin took the proffered chair and sat. "No, thank you, Don Fioretti. I *have* already eaten."

"And you look like a scarecrow. So little meat on your bones. Please, let me at least get you a bowl of ravioli."

"Of course."

"And wine," Fioretti called to one of the waitresses.

Lyons waited and watched as Turrin sat silently until he was served. He couldn't help but admire the little Fed's aplomb. Lyons had pulled undercover work occasionally, even since joining Able Team, but he'd never been in as deep as Turrin.

"So," Fioretti said as Turrin spooned up some of the steaming ravioli, "what brings you to me?"

Turrin blotted his lips with a napkin. "The ravioli is good. Hot." He picked up the wineglass. "The wine, also, is excellent. I thank you for your hospitality, Don Fioretti."

The old man made a gesture of dismissal.

"Sadly my reason for being here is bad business."

Fioretti glared across the table. His hand curled into a fist. "And the author of this bad business?"

"None other than yourself, Don Fioretti."

A crimson blush stained the old Don's face. The four torpedoes shifted uneasily.

"You dare," Fioretti asked in a hoarse whisper, "you dare come to my restaurant, eat at my table and accuse me of bad business within the space of a few heartbeats?"

Turrin's face remained impassive. He rested his hands on the table. Lyons noted in satisfaction that the little Fed's hand was within inches of the sharp knife that had been brought out with his meal. If necessary, it could provide a few seconds of distraction.

"I didn't come here," Turrin replied. "I was *sent*."

Fioretti leaned back in his chair and snapped his fingers again.

The spindly old restaurant manager trotted forward, locked the entrance and turned the Open sign around so it read Closed. He wiped his hands on his apron nervously as he made his way back to the counter.

"Who sent you?" Fioretti asked.

"La Commissione," Turrin stated, then speared another ravioli.

Fioretti spread his hands. "La Commissione has only little power since Mack the Bastard chewed through their ranks."

Turrin didn't bat an eye. "They still have enough to send me here. If necessary, they'll send more."

"And you, Leo, where do you fit into this?"

"I'm only a messenger."

"You know what the Romans did to messengers bearing bad news, don't you?" a young man sitting at the table with the bodyguard asked.

Turrin grinned. "Yeah, kid, I do. But you should see what the Colombians do to them. Me, I'm not impressed by Romans."

The young man stood. His chair spilled over backward and clattered against the wooden floor. "You son of a bitch!" His hand darted under his suit coat.

Lyons touched the butt of the .45 under his jacket.

Turrin speared another ravioli and chewed it in idle speculation.

"Nicky!" Fioretti's voice was a hoarse roar of displeasure.

"Grandfather," the young man said, "this man has insulted you. He has insulted our family. You should throw him out on his ass, if you choose to let him live at all."

"Nicky, sit down."

The younger Fioretti remained standing.

"Nicky." Fioretti's voice was neutral, and he didn't look at his grandson. "If I have to tell you again, I'll have Sal break your legs so you'll remember to obey more easily in the future."

Nick Fioretti sat.

The old man leaned forward and rested his elbows on the table. "Talk, Leo. Convince me of some reason why I should let you leave this place still breathing."

"Actually," Turrin said, "one main reason is that I would make a terrible antipasto in an otherwise good restaurant."

A tense silence followed, then was broken by Fioretti's wheezing gales of laughter. He slapped the table in his mirth. "Ah, Leo, do they still cling to those old stories about me?"

Turrin finished chewing and swallowed. "Yes, Don Fioretti, but only at times and politely these days." He gestured toward the plate before him. "As you can see, though, I don't believe those stories."

Fioretti waved toward the wine bottle, and one of the men refilled the glasses. "So, you work for La Commissione these days?"

"No. Mostly I'm retired. Occasionally I can be asked to do a favor."

"Angelina and the children?"

"In good health. It's kind of you to ask."

"Family, Leo, these are the important things in life. Unlike so many others, you know this."

"Yes."

"But the cowboy you have with you," Fioretti said, pointing at Lyons, "he isn't of the blood."

"No, but he has all the heart he'll ever need."

"This is one bad thing that has happened. We've lost so much of the true blood of our people."

"It's only one thing among many."

"I think it will be the one that will eventually kill us, though. These Japanese and Colombians, they make doing business even harder. They're like those piranha fish, devouring each other if no one else is available. Now, even some of our own are emulating these people."

"I understand."

"Maybe you were wise to step down from a position of power when you did."

"I had no choice," Turrin said. "The OrgCrime Task Force was closing in on me. Rather than fight that, I opted to sit on the sidelines and do the occasional favor when I could."

"And this favor now?"

"There's a passport business, Don Fioretti. It operates somewhere in Brooklyn, but I've been told it's known to you or your people."

"If so, what does it have to do with La Commissione?"

"The people in this business, they're providing passports and new identification papers to the Arab terrorists in this country."

Lyons watched Fioretti's face for a response. A tic started under the bag of the left eye.

"This is a heavy accusation. How sure are you of your sources?"

Turrin pushed his plate away. "I respect you, Don Fioretti. I wouldn't be here if I wasn't sure of the truth."

"And what does La Commissione want?"

"The business found and destroyed. The people who are responsible, to be destroyed with it. We don't want any of this business with the terrorists traced back to our Families."

Lyons was sure the action was going to start any second. Turrin had stepped over every boundary regarding the man's self-worth.

Instead, Fioretti leaned back in his chair and touched his lips with his napkin. He spoke without looking. "Nicky? What do you know of this passport business?"

"Nothing, Grandfather. I think this man has come here to throw garbage over our name." Nicky Fioretti gave Turrin a hard stare, then shared it with Lyons.

The Able Team warrior let a hint of laughter light his eyes.

Nicky Fioretti's face darkened with anger.

"Don Fioretti," the man to the old man's right said politely. He leaned forward and whispered into Fioretti's ear. The old Don's face shifted from neutral to bleak and stony. His gaze remained locked on Turrin.

"Nicky," Fioretti said in a cold whisper, "you will tell Leo what you know of this passport business in Brooklyn."

Nicky Fioretti faced the older man. "You're weak, Grandfather, if you choose blood over family. This man comes in here and makes wild accusations, and you believe him. Maybe it is time the Fioretti Family was nurtured by a new and stronger guiding hand."

Everything seemed to come apart at once. It was so instant that Lyons figured the plans had been in the works for a while.

Three of the four standing guards evidently belonged to Nicky Fioretti. One of them killed the fourth man where he stood while the other two turned their weapons toward Lyons.

On the move, the Able warrior dropped into a roll as bullets tore splinters from the polished floor. He had the .45 in his hand, felt it buck when his sights fell into place. He spaced the clip two shots to a man, aimed for the chest and hoped none of them wore Kevlar vests. By the time he got to his feet, he'd traded the .45 for the .357. The hammer spur eared back with a harsh click.

The movement continued at the table, and Lyons caught it from the corner of his eye.

The man sitting to Turrin's right reached under his jacket. Without hesitation the stocky little Fed gripped the steak knife and ripped it across the man's throat. While still seated, he placed a foot in the man's chest and kicked man and chair both over to sprawl on the floor. His other hand came out holding one of the .38 Bodyguards.

Nicky Fioretti was obviously distressed by the turn of events. His hand moved no more than inches. Then Don Fioretti seized the meat fork from the table and plunged it through his grandson's hand into the table. Nicky screamed and yanked, moving the table only slightly before realizing he'd been nailed to it.

Fioretti kept his hand on the meat fork and stared into his grandson's tearing eyes. "I do this for the blood and for family, you little lying fuck. If your father were alive today, God rest his soul, he'd kill you with his own hands. Dealing with these terrorists is worse than prostituting yourself for the Crips and Bloods. I'm shamed to have you carry my son's name."

Lyons checked the four guards scattered across the floor. None of them were alive. He caught Nicky Fioretti's look of wild anticipation as he glanced back toward the kitchen. The old man and the three waitresses had dived to cover behind the counter.

He raised the Python as two shapes stepped through the swing doors separating the dining room from the kitchen. When he recognized Schwarz and Blancanales, he lowered the pistol.

Turrin dropped the bloody knife on the corpse at his side.

Don Fioretti waggled the meat fork. His grandson cringed in pain. "Talk, Nicky, or I swear you'll be days in the dying."

"Okay, okay, just take the fork out."

Fioretti nodded, and the man at his side got up and removed his grandson's pistols. With a swift yank, he freed the meat fork.

The younger man groaned and fell forward onto the table. He cradled his injured hand against his chest.

"The address," Turrin said.

"Nicky," Fioretti warned.

Lyons memorized it when it came out in choked gasps.

"It isn't their permanent address," the young man added, "but I've met their representatives there."

Don Fioretti crossed his arms over his barrel chest and sat up straight in the chair. "Leo, I could help you in this."

"No, thank you, Don Fioretti, but this is something I've been assigned to take care of on the qt."

Fioretti nodded his head. "I understand."

"If you could see to it that no word of this reaches the streets..."

"Of course. Whomever my grandson has pulled to his side in this matter, they'll know to stay out of it or feel my wrath, as well."

Turrin pocketed his .38 and stood to go.

"You'll allow me the respect of cleaning my own house, Leo?"

"Of course. La Commissione has never found fault with you or your operations. Nor will they now."

Fioretti bowed his head in silent thanks.

Turrin reached out a hand, took Fioretti's and kissed the man's ring. His face was impassive.

Keeping the Python in his hand, Lyons followed Turrin out the door. Nicky Fioretti's sullen look burned into him. At the other end of the restaurant, Blancanales and Schwarz faded into the kitchen.

Outside, Lyons put the Python away and slid behind the wheel of the rental car. No one followed them from the restaurant. Picking up the ear-throat headset, he hit the transmit button. "Pol? Gadgets?"

"Here, Ironman. We're rolling. You just name the place."

Lyons did, then cleared. He put the car in gear and moved into the flow of traffic. "You see a lot of that when you were inside the organization, Leo?"

"Yeah."

"Ever get used to it?"

"No."

Lyons massaged the back of his neck with a big hand. "Gives me the creeps."

"Me, too." Turrin took out a pack of cigarettes and shook one loose. He lit it and expelled a puff of smoke. "Still," he said, looking at Lyons, "I'd rather go up against guys like Fioretti and his grandson than the people we're after. At least I can understand the Mafia. I know why they do what they do, and I know how far they'll go to get it done."

A brief memory of the terrorist in the hospital who'd cut his own throat flashed through Lyons's mind. "They go the distance, Leo," he said softly. "Like nobody else you've ever seen."

9

A small army rose up from the desert dust scarcely fifty yards from Mack Bolan's jeep. He killed the engine and let the vehicle coast to a stop. The transmission whined as it slowed.

The black dragonfly shape of an Apache gunship lifted into the air, swirled briefly against the purple clouds gathered along the eastern edge of the sandy world, then settled into an approach pattern that left the jeep defenseless before its guns. The pilot used the rising morning sun as part of his shield.

Jack Grimaldi shifted uneasily in the passenger seat.

Snugging his ear-throat headset into place, Bolan tapped the transmit button. "Desert Lightning Base, this is Desert Lightning One. Over."

"This is Desert Lightning Base, Desert Lightning One. With all due respect, sir, we'll need to see your bona fides before you proceed any farther. Over."

"Desert Lightning Base, come ahead. Desert Lightning One out." Bolan hung up the mike.

The Apache helicopter flew closer, armament bristling from all sides. It settled into hover mode and tilted down to cover the jeep easily.

The soldier who approached the jeep was young. Bolan looked at the man and tried to remember if he'd ever been that young in war. He knew that he had. He and Grimaldi placed their hands in the open on the dashboard. The rifle barrel confronting them didn't waver.

After firing off a salute, the soldier slung his M-16 and reached out a hand.

Bolan passed over the requested documents. Dressed as they were in desert camouflage and rigged out in combat harnesses and M-16s, he knew he and Grimaldi fit in easily.

Satisfied, the soldier passed the portfolio back. "A pleasure to serve under you, Colonel Pollock. Welcome to Operation Desert Lightning. You'll find the main camp seven klicks farther south. Lieutenant Colonel Eldridge is expecting you, sir."

Bolan nodded and engaged the jeep's transmission.

"Desert Lightning One, this is Desert Lightning Base. You have the all clear. Out."

There was no road, but as Bolan passed he saw men hunkered down under small tents that blunted the harsh desert heat. Fighting holes were black against the tan-colored sand.

"God," Grimaldi said in a harsh whisper over the drone of the jeep's transmission, "most of these guys are just kids."

"Yeah, and you can bet the guys who had twenty-year hash marks when we went in said the same thing about us."

"I know, but you'd think after a while we could stop giving up our young men to war."

A fatigue-clad form that definitely wasn't male drew the attention of both men.

"And young women," Grimaldi amended. "This war has seen some changes."

Bolan silently agreed. And yet some things never changed. He glanced at the young faces surrounding them, the weapons held so casually in hands that hadn't so long ago put away schoolbooks to spend summers under a more pleasant sun.

"You're looking at the downside of it," the Executioner said. "Think back, Jack. Remember why you joined, why you went to Vietnam?"

"I felt I was needed."

"These men and women felt they were needed, too." The jeep angled off down an unseen incline in a cloud of dust.

Grimaldi freed a pair of handkerchiefs, and they tied them over their lower faces. It helped, but the dust seemed to seep through somehow anyway.

Bolan killed the jeep's engine and coasted to a stop in front of the command post. It wasn't marked, but he recognized Lieutenant Colonel Joshua Eldridge from the briefing at Stony Man Farm. The eight other men standing with him were of various rank.

"Atten-tion!" Eldridge bellowed.

The officers formed a line and held their salute.

Bolan clambered from the jeep, came to attention with an ease that had become as much a part of him as breathing over the years. He saluted, maintained his attitude of a superior officer because it was something these troops expected. To not show it would be to confuse them. And with something in the neighborhood of eighteen hundred soldiers under his command in what could quickly become threatened territory, confusion was the last thing he wanted.

"At ease," Bolan ordered as he came to a stop facing Eldridge. The man was easily three inches taller than Bolan's six-foot-three, and was at least fifty pounds heavier. The lieutenant colonel's uniform was immaculate.

"Lieutenant Colonel Joshua Eldridge at your service, Colonel Pollock."

"Thank you, Colonel." Bolan hooked a thumb over his shoulder and indicated Grimaldi. "I'd like you to meet Captain Graves. He'll be operating as my personal liaison during this present series of missions."

"Yes, sir. It's a pleasure to meet you, Captain."

Introductions were quickly made concerning the other officers. Bolan didn't try to remember them. The time would come when it would be necessary, but nearly everything would be passed down through Eldridge.

Pocketing his sunglasses, Bolan followed the lieutenant colonel into the command post tent, which covered a twenty-by-twenty space. A thin carpet covered the sand and gave way spongily underfoot. Tables lined the four sides of the tent and the center of the available room. A radio operator came to attention beside his hardware.

Bolan acknowledged the man with a salute and ordered him at ease.

Eldridge switched on a light hanging overhead. "An interesting bit of information has just come to us within the hour, Colonel." He gestured toward the tables in the center of the room. "According to our local sources, there's an Iraqi terrorist communications center operating in northern Kuwait. They're the ones who ran the assault against UN forces thirty-nine hours ago."

Bolan studied the array of satellite pictures overlaid by see-through graphs marking off military quadrants. "Has that been confirmed?"

"Yes, sir." Eldridge placed his forefinger on one of the maps. "It's near Multa, about eleven klicks away, situated in the Kraal al-Mura region."

"There are foothills in that area, sir," one of Eldridge's captains said. "Presumably those Intelligence people could hole up indefinitely and cause all kinds of damage to our people still in the area. Missile launchings at this time could strike critical areas of allied holdings, cost the lives of possibly hundreds more people."

"We were discussing ways of rooting them out when you arrived," Eldridge said. "Assuming they've dug themselves in and fortified their position, an air strike isn't the answer."

"I agree." Bolan looked at Eldridge. "What did you have in mind?"

"Team deployment, sir." Eldridge clasped his hands behind his back. "I've got some people who're highly trained in counterterrorism. If we give them the specs, I have no doubt that they could infiltrate the area and eliminate the opposition."

"Sounds good to me," Bolan said, "but I'll be fielding my own team of specialists."

The commanders swapped uncertain looks.

"Sir?" Eldridge said. "I was told you'd be taking over operations here, Colonel."

"I am," Bolan said. He glanced up at the man and held the gaze. "But I'm not at liberty to tell you everything else I'm involved with."

"Of course, sir." Eldridge's ears turned crimson. The other men diplomatically looked back at the satellite pictures.

"I'll need everything you can assemble regarding this terrorist outpost," Bolan went on. "Your major can see to the details."

"Yes, sir."

"And Major?"

"Yes, sir."

"I want those facts and figures available and on my desk in twenty-two minutes. At 0700 hours."

"Yes, sir." The major snapped a salute and began gathering materials.

"Corporal?"

The communications officer came to attention beside his gear. "Yes, sir."

"Captain Graves will assist you in placing some telecommunications. Make sure he makes his connections with all due haste."

"Yes sir."

"Captain Graves."

"On my way, Colonel." Grimaldi gave him a salute and executed a neat quarter turn despite the loose carpet.

"Colonel Eldridge, I'd like you to escort me to my quarters."

"Yes, sir." Eldridge's eyes stared at the tent wall over Bolan's shoulder.

"The rest of you men are dismissed until further notice."

They saluted and left.

Bolan followed Eldridge out of the tent, paused at the jeep to gather his personal effects and a thermos, then went across the wide space separating them from the next row, three tents down, and inside a small tent. With the flap closed, the air inside felt dead and still. Perspiration trickled down the big warrior's back.

Eldridge stood at attention just inside the door.

The tent didn't provide luxurious accommodations. A cot lined one wall with light sheets neatly folded over it. The desk was a small affair of pine and aluminum below a bulletin board secured to a tent wall. A thin carpet covered the floor.

Bolan tossed his duffel beside the cot, unslung his M-16 and put it on top of the cot. He shook the thermos. It was a full one he and Grimaldi had packed back in Kuwait. He kept his back to Eldridge, remembering that assuming command from another person was never easy. Too much pride went into the job, and from the reports he'd seen on Eldridge, little of the man didn't belong lock, stock and barrel to the military.

"At ease," Bolan said. He heard Eldridge move behind him, knew before he turned around that the man would only allow himself to fall into parade rest. He found a stack of disposable cups by the pitcher of warm water in his personal supplies. "Would you like some coffee?"

"No, sir. Permission to speak freely, sir?"

Bolan turned around, a cup of coffee in his fist.

Eldridge's eyes burned.

"No," Bolan said bluntly. "I don't think that would be a good idea."

Eldridge kept his eyes focused over Bolan's shoulder.

"You don't like me," Bolan said. "I came here to take over an operation you feel you should be in command of. There's no way to rectify that to you, so I won't waste my time or breath trying. Our country is at war, and bickering over bureaucratic niceties is *not* a worthwhile pursuit. I'm here to put an end to hostile aggression as quickly as possible. While I'm in command here, you will respond to whatever duties I assign you to the best of your abilities. Is that understood?''

"Yes, sir."

"There'll be parts of the campaign that you'll deliberately be kept in the dark about. If told to keep your questions to yourself and any personal inquiries from those operations, you'll do so."

"Yes, sir."

"You will *not* seek to discover who these other agencies are, or what they are doing here."

"No, sir."

"I tell you this now so you don't have to guess. I respect you, Eldridge. You've got a long and distinguished career with the Army and the Special Forces. However, these are extenuating circumstances." Bolan sipped his coffee. "Is there anything else we need to discuss that doesn't fall into those parameters?"

"No, sir."

"Then you're dismissed, soldier."

"Thank you, sir." Eldridge saluted, did an about-face and left without another word.

Bolan took out his map case and spread topographical survey maps of Kuwait across his desk. He hated being so rough on Eldridge, but there had been no other way to handle it. A sign of weakness on his part could have splintered the working relationship before it had a chance to get going. And failure here could be measured in lives.

Grimaldi entered the tent less than two minutes later. "I saw Eldridge outside. I take it you didn't win any friends with your dazzling conversation."

"No."

"I got hold of Barb and Aaron through the secure line. Talia Alireza had some problems in Bahrain, but she's in Kuwait City waiting on us."

"What problems?"

"She didn't go into it."

"She and her team are still operational?"

"Yes."

"Could Aaron help us out with the topography in Kraal al-Mura?"

"We'll get it as soon as he's got it." Grimaldi checked his watch. "A satellite's supposed to be over that area in thirty-one minutes. When you referred to your own 'team of specialists,' I'm assuming you were talking about Alireza and her people?"

Bolan nodded. "It serves two purposes. It eliminates the probability of the Iraqis finding out about the military ground team we've got fielded here because of troop movement."

"And it gives us a look at what Alireza and her group are made of."

"Yeah."

"I got a hunch the next few days are going to be mighty interesting," Grimaldi said.

Bolan finished his coffee. "I'm thinking the first few hours are going to tell us a lot. If we have to wait days, we're going to be even further behind the terrorist network and Shawiyya.''

EVERY TIME Yakov Katzenelenbogen saw the Wailing Wall, a sense of awe filled him. It was so now. Dozens of men—some clothed in the black suits that were the way of Hasidic Jews with their beards and long hair, and others dressed more conventionally—stood before the mammoth limestone blocks that had once made up the western wall of the courtyard surrounding the temple. Many of the men stood silently in prayer or kissed the stones or thrust written prayers into the cracks between the blocks.

To Katz, the wall was a testimony of a people—*his* people—to weather centuries of abuse and war. He took strength from it, added its resolve to his own, then walked on. He'd die before he watched it fall.

The alleys were twisting and narrow here. Few streets existed that would permit cars to pass. Waves of people moved to one side or the other as donkeys pulled carts of goods and foodstuffs to and fro. Morning's shadows clung to the masonry surrounding the tide of men and women. The sun hadn't yet warmed the air sliding through the breezeways. Crisp and cool still, it carried a rush of odors—coffees, spices, roasting lambs, hashish, perfumes, soaps, leathers, all manner of things that brought memories to mind. He'd lived here for a time, and he'd been happy.

But that happiness was in the past.

He put his thoughts away, focused on his present mission here.

"Katz?"

Thumbing the transmit button on his ear-throat headset, Katz responded. "Here." He turned his head toward the alley wall so no one could hear his words.

"We might have a problem, mate," McCarter replied. "Calvin just made a group of clandestine types moving in your direction. Could be we're not the only ones who turned up this little terrorist love nest."

"Stay out of their way," Katz radioed back. "Any kind of trouble here could ignite the powder keg around us."

"I read you. But you bloody well better be ready to weigh anchor should the time arrive because we didn't come this far to leave you hanging."

"I understand."

Katz found the bakery sign he was searching for, then walked past it and climbed the narrow stone steps leading up. The smell of fresh bread followed him to the second and third floors. Gloom seemed to seep from the cracks between the irregularly spaced rocks making up the walls. The wrought-iron railing tilted under his hand and squeaked once when he touched it. He abandoned the railing and trusted his footing. He was counting on silence to achieve his mission.

Manning's voice echoed in his ear. "You need to snap to it, Katz. There's an Israeli army contingent headed that way now. I count eighteen men in uniform, and they're not exactly receiving a standing ovation from the crowds.''

Drawing the Beretta 92-F from a hip holster under his sports coat, Katz leaned into the pace. He had the hook in place on his prosthesis because it would be more serviceable than the artificial hand. The man he came for wouldn't go willingly.

On the third-floor landing, he concealed the pistol behind his thigh as he walked. He peered around the corner, back in Manning's direction. He caught a glimpse of the Israeli soldiers jumping out of the deuce-and-a-half four blocks away. They moved out at once, elbowing their way through the crowds. Curses in a half-dozen languages flowed in their wake.

The Phoenix leader didn't waste time trying to guess how Israeli Intelligence had tumbled to the hidden terrorists. It had taken two hours of intensive work for the team to track down the leads provided by Kurtzman and Price. They'd been aware of the net the Mossad had spread throughout the West Bank, as well. It was possible they'd led the Israelis to the terrorists themselves.

At the door he shoved his Beretta under his right arm, reached into his jacket pocket for a lock pick and picked the door. He rested his hook on the doorknob to keep the door closed, then took up his pistol once more. Pressing an ear to the door, he heard voices inside. He identified a man's, then a woman's, talking softly, laughing together.

He visualized the apartment in his mind again. The door opened into a living-room-bedroom combination. A small kitchenette sat off to the left. A bathroom was to the right. He'd let himself into a neighboring apartment only a few minutes ago to familiarize himself with the layout.

Katz hit the door with a shoulder and followed it inside. The pistol came up automatically.

Acrid smoke from burning candles stung his eyes. The candle flames themselves barely cut through the gloom filling the room. A curtain of strung beads and bells separated the living-room-bedroom from the kitchenette, and clacked and clinked from the breeze spilling in through the partially open window on the opposite wall. The strong smell of burning incense swirled in the gray smoke drifting through the open door.

A half-naked woman straddled a man lying back on a battered plaid couch piled with pillows. Her skin was dusky olive. The expression on her face turned from surprise to fear, and she brought up her hands to cover her bare breasts. The man's hands were high up under her skirt on the outside of her hips. His face became a grimace of hate. The scar over his right eye confirmed his identity as Sofian Nejd, the man Katz had come seeking.

"Katz," McCarter called in Katzenelenbogen's ear, "the plainclothes group has made your building. They're mounting the steps now, mate."

Katz didn't try to respond. He was aware of the buzz of voices in the alley below. Before he could speak to the couple, the man's right hand emerged from the shelter of the skirt holding a 9 mm pistol.

Throwing himself to one side, Katz smashed into the wall beside the door. A picture of a marketplace scene fell from the wall and smashed against the floor. Four shots drilled into the wall just behind the Phoenix Force leader.

Katz lifted his pistol, started to pull the trigger with the sights on the terrorist's left shoulder. He was forced to stop when the terrorist shoved the woman at him.

She screamed and flailed as she stumbled backward, her screams becoming Arabic curses when she collided with Katz. No longer flailing helplessly, her arms and hands smashed against his face, her sharp nails clawing for his eyes.

The terrorist jumped up from the couch and leveled his weapon.

With a formidable backhand, Katz swept the woman from his line of fire using his prosthesis as a club. He fired a heartbeat after the terrorist. Wind from the 9 mm bullet blew hotly across his face. His round took the terrorist in his gun arm and spilled the weapon to the floor while it drove the man backward.

The woman hissed and screeched when Katz stepped over her. Footsteps sounded on the stone stairs outside. Anxious voices spoke rapidly, grew closer.

Katz was only dimly aware of them. He placed a foot on the fallen pistol as the terrorist dived for it. His other foot came across in a wicked *savate* kick and knocked the man backward.

The terrorist thumped solidly against a small table. It held for only a moment, then came apart in a crash of ripping wood.

"Alive," Katz said in Arabic. "Dead, you're no use to me." He held the Beretta muzzle centered on the man's face.

"Jewish cur," Nejd snarled through split lips. Blood trickled down his beard, spattering against his white shirt. His eyes flashed with animal cunning as he climbed slowly to his feet. "You think you can get a warrior of the true and great jihad to spill his mind to unclean vermin?"

Katz let the silent movement of the Beretta be his answer.

With a cry of fear and rage, the terrorist threw himself at Katz.

The Phoenix Force leader moved and easily dodged the man's advance. He swung his prosthesis, felt the vibration as the steel frame thunked solidly into the back of Nejd's skull.

The woman raised herself from the floor and attacked Katz. Nejd took the opportunity to make for the door. In the time it took Katz to free himself from the woman, the terrorist froze less than a yard outside the door, then returned just as quickly as he'd left. He gazed about wildly, then screamed with the loss of all hope. Ignoring Katz and the struggling woman, Nejd streaked for the window at the other end of the room.

The man never paused. He crossed his arms in front of his face as he threw himself through the window. Glass shattered and went to pieces all around him. He sailed outward for a few yards before succumbing to the call of gravity. Then he dropped like a rock.

Katz shoved the woman from him. She fell onto the couch and wept with high, keening moans. Reaching the broken window, Katz peered down.

Nejd's body lay spread-eagled on the cobblestone alley below. From the various angles of the limbs, it appeared several bones had been broken from the impact. No sign of life was evident.

"Katz!" McCarter sounded frustrated.

Footsteps sounded just outside the door.

Katz glanced down the irregular wall. There was no way down except through the front. He tapped the transmit button. "Get yourself and the others clear, David. The trail has ended here. Good hunting."

"Get out of there."

"There's no time, my friend," Katz said as he turned to face the armed men coming in through the door. "No time at all."

"IT ISN'T SO BAD," the KGB doctor said in solemn tones as he applied a new bandage.

Hamoud Jaluwi looked at the man impassively despite the pounding headache that seemed to be attempting to give birth between his temples. Cool air filled the Russian jet. White clouds pooled outside the round windows. Less than a dozen hard-faced men occupied the four rows of seats, leaving many empty ones between them. Assault rifles and other weapons remained within easy reach of their owners.

"That's easy for you to say," Jaluwi said in Russian. "You weren't the one so greviously injured."

"It isn't so bad," the doctor insisted in tones that said he clearly understood his professional skills were in question.

"And if it scars?" Jaluwi demanded as he touched the bandage on the left side of his forehead.

The doctor opened his mouth to respond.

"And if it scars," Another Russian voice said from behind Jaluwi, "it will only add character to the rugged face of a new world leader."

Jaluwi glanced up.

Semyon Zagladin stood in the aisle between the double rows of seats. He was more dapper than a big man had any right to be. His suit fit him well without signs of obvious tailoring to achieve the effect. Although he was well-groomed, his hands were rough and weathered.

The hands of a farmer, Jaluwi had reflected occasionally during their relationship. He still remembered his father's hands—hard, and callused and scarred, blunted by the erosion of time, black nails always torn and jagged. Zagladin had been a surprise. Jaluwi hadn't expected a farmer to be so devious.

"There are many women who liked my face just as it was," Jaluwi said.

"And many more who will now welcome you into their embraces, my friend. After all, will you not be known as the man who saved the whole of the Middle East from the Great Satans in the West?" Zagladin sat down beside Jaluwi.

"Still, this shouldn't have happened. I shouldn't have been harmed."

"No, you're right. We should have waited for the Americans to figure out who was behind the terrorist attacks and actually had you shot down." Zagladin's gray eyes turned flinty. "These people aren't fools, comrade. We can fool all of them perhaps some of the time, but not all of them all of the time."

"Now you quote American television comedians at me."

Zagladin smiled. "Only when it's true." He laced his fingers and rested them in his lap. "With you dead, perhaps you can hope to live longer as the Americans and their allies piece together the puzzle before them."

Jaluwi glanced out the window. The red light over the doorway to the cabin flashed and signaled for the occupants to fasten their seat belts.

"We used the best props we could find," Zagladin said as he secured his belt. "It's too bad we were unable to trust one of the special-effects people we bought the materials from to do the job themselves. Still, I think it was a good production. It has been on the news worldwide for almost fourteen hours now.

Much public sentiment has been successfully aroused in Syria and the other sympathetic countries.''

Touching the bandage again, Jaluwi remembered the explosive pop of the fake wound when the detonator went off on cue. The concussion had torn his flesh to the bone in a three-inch split, peppered his skin and the wound with traces of black powder that he knew might never fade. Vertigo had assailed his senses for hours afterward.

He studied his colorless reflection in the window. He had a narrow face with generous features. Women *had* commented on how handsome he was. Perhaps a scar wouldn't be so bad. Then they could make observations about how brave he was. They'd never have to know that the assassin's bullet had been faked.

"What of Khalid Shawiyya?" Jaluwi asked.

"He's waiting for us," Zagladin replied.

"He knows nothing of my arrival?"

"No. The KGB is just as aware as you are of Shawiyya's faults as a braggart. If he even suspected you were alive, there'd be no way we could keep up this deception."

Jaluwi smiled in satisfaction. "My spies have told me of Shawiyya's intentions to find the owner of the voice that commands him over the phone and kill him, then take his place." He laughed. "Even if they weren't under orders to watch him as closely as they are, Shawiyya's plans would be known to me. The man is as heavy-handed and as lacking in finesse as his predecessor. He has no imagination outside of feeding his own ego."

The jet angled in for a landing.

Jaluwi watched the airfield come up to meet them. He tightened his fingers in his seat harness as the wheels shrieked across the hot tarmac. Once the landing had been completed and they were taxiing toward a sheet-metal hangar, Jaluwi got up and fell in behind the first two Russian guards standing by the exit.

The Russians hit the release bars and let the door out, then walked into the open carefully with their AK-47s at the ready.

Jaluwi followed.

Light dimmed as the double doors of the hangar were closed after a jeep had been allowed through.

Zagladin stepped in front of Jaluwi. The jeep came to a rocking stop only a few yards from the Russians. Behind the big KGB agent, Jaluwi knew he couldn't be seen.

Khalid Shawiyya climbed out of the passenger seat with a look of self-importance filling his round face. He threw his arms wide and said, "Let me be the first to welcome you to my country."

Zagladin said nothing, merely stepped aside to reveal Jaluwi.

Drawing the 9 mm pistol from inside his jacket smoothly, Jaluwi thrust it before him and aimed it at Shawiyya.

"You!" Shawiyya exclaimed as he reached for the Detonics .45 sheathed on his hip.

"Yes," Jaluwi replied, squeezing the trigger four times. The bullets struck the Iraqi president in the chest and punched his body backward.

"Help me!" Shawiyya ordered. He held a hand across his chest to slow the bleeding, then reached for the .45 that lay only inches away from his outstretched hand.

The Iraqi guards did nothing.

Jaluwi walked forward, kicked the .45 away from Shawiyya, then squatted. He smiled when he saw the anger firing deep inside the Iraqi president's eyes. "I see you aren't a complete fool, Shawiyya."

"You've been the one on the phone," Shawiyya said.

"Yes."

"I could have killed you." Shawiyya's hand clutched at the spreading pools of blood covering his chest. "You are nothing. Nothing!"

"And you're a fool who followed on the heels of another fool to a position of power neither of you deserved. You've used the Arab people for your own ends. That's why no one will lift a finger to help you. I come to lead them into a more deserving existence. You'd only guide them through more shadow and more needless death."

Shawiyya spit bloody phlegm.

Wiping the spittle from his chest, Jaluwi said, "My only regret is that you have but one life to give for your country." He pointed the pistol between Shawiyya's eyes and pulled the trigger.

WINDING THROUGH the bowels of the wreckage of Kuwait City, Bolan kept his M-16 folded across his chest. He was togged out in a combat blacksuit, with the Desert Eagle riding at his hip and the Beretta 93-R in shoulder leather. His combat harness and webbing held other weapons of war.

A burst of static raced across the frequency his earthroat headset was tuned on.

Even though the noonday sun burned down relentlessly, the jumbled slabs of concrete from collapsed buildings held pockets of night black. The street the buildings had once fronted no longer existed. Pockmarked pavement was flanked here and there by shattered curbing. Crushed and stripped cars lay scattered under the wreckage.

Bolan stepped over a fallen light pole, managed a loose wedge of brick wall that teetered unexpectedly underfoot and went on. He was aware of the other people scattered throughout the area even though he hadn't seen them or allowed himself to be seen by them. The problem remained, though, whether they were friend or foe.

Talia Alireza was known to him by sight from the Stony Man files. The rest of her team were virtual unknowns.

"Striker." It was a woman's voice.

Bolan thumbed the transmit button. "Here."

"How many are you?"

"Two."

"I count more men than that." Her voice was calm, professional.

"So do I."

"Who are they?"

"I haven't gotten close enough to confirm an ID. I was thinking they were yours."

"No."

"Then we have a problem." Bolan came to a halt with his back against the cracked foundation of an office building. Perspiration covered his body, made the blacksuit cling to him even more tightly. Using his peripheral vision to pick up movement, he wiped his palms and resecured his grip on the assault rifle.

"The integrity of your operation leaves much to be desired," the woman said sarcastically.

Bolan ignored the gibe. "I was told you'd have a word for me."

"If our meeting place was blown, don't you imagine they could have the rest of it?" The woman sighed, then gave the password.

Bolan gave her the countersign, then added another code word. He thumbed the transmit button. "Jack?"

"Already made the change, guy," Grimaldi replied.

The Executioner reached into his webbing and pulled out a crimson scarf from among a selection of yellow, white and green ones. He tied it around his upper left arm. With that in place, he, Grimaldi, Talia

Alireza and her people would be clearly identified to one another.

He moved quietly, tracking the movement he'd spotted from the corner of his eye. Until they'd managed to secure or leave the area undetected, he knew Alireza's mercenary band wouldn't make contact with Grimaldi or him. He stepped through a jagged crack that had once been a window and drew the silenced Beretta with his right hand.

Two men in black cammies held a position inside the partially demolished building. Neither wore the crimson armband that denoted a friendly, and they carried AK-47s. One man had a backpack rigging hung with a pair of LAWs.

Bolan advanced on them from out of the shadows, the 93-R held rock steady before him. "Hey," he said softly. Fragments of concrete, mortar, brick and glass were spread out over the wide floor before him.

Both men moved immediately, bringing their weapons to their shoulders.

For an instant their faces froze in the Executioner's view. They were lighter complected than Arabs, but didn't hold a true European look, having more of a Slavic cast.

One of the men muttered a curse in Russian.

Bolan squeezed the Beretta's trigger. The round took the man through the forehead and slammed him back against the wall. The second man got off a short burst that dug up stone splinters from the floor only a few feet in front of the big warrior. A pair of 9 mm

parabellums punched through his heart and left his
corpse sprawled over a small concrete glacier.

Ears still ringing from the autofire, Bolan advanced on the pair of men. He knelt and started going through their pockets. His mind recalled the curse
in Russian, turned it over and over and tried to fit it in
with what he knew of the terrorist activity. But there
was nothing to tie it to.

A long, lean shadow fell across the window Bolan
had entered. He spun, Beretta in his fist as he leveled
it out before him.

The figure in the dark cammies was feminine. Talia's tawny hair was tied back, and she carried a cut-
down Remington Model 870 shotgun in her gloved
hands.

"Striker?" she asked.

Bolan nodded, then slid the 93-R back into leather
and continued to rifle the pockets of the dead men.

Talia approached him. "Russians," she said after
a look.

"I think so." Bolan gave up the search. Neither man
had anything in the way of identification.

"They are," Talia said with conviction.

He stood and looked at her. "What makes you so
sure?"

"You see the same things I do. Do you doubt the
evidence your eyes tell you?"

"Even if they are Russian, they could be indepen-
dents in this."

"And be into our Intelligence network?" Talia shook her head. "Not unless you people are using primitive equipment. I checked. I couldn't find out about you. Your mission controller went to great lengths to persuade me she was for real. No, these men are KGB agents. I ran into one in Bahrain." She slung the shotgun, slipped a small camera from a pack at the back of her waist and took pictures of the men, including frontals and profiles. "Maybe, if we live long enough, we can find out who they belong to."

Bolan was suddenly aware of the vibration beneath the soles of his boots that was steadily growing stronger. "Tank," he said.

Talia put the camera away, fisted the shotgun again and led the way out of the ruined building.

The receiver in Bolan's ear crackled as he knotted a fist in the backpack containing the LAWs.

"Incoming!" Jack Grimaldi's voice warned.

Bolan heard the shrill whistle of approaching missiles cutting through the air as soon as he broke free of the building.

"Scuds!" he announced.

The missiles blistered the air overhead, drowned out the approach of the tank in the explosions. The ground shook. Wedges of concrete and brick went sliding over each other, became an obstacle course.

Autofire blasted shattered window fragments from a compact car lying over on its side near Bolan and his companion.

The Executioner followed the mercenary leader to ground beside the vehicle. He thumbed the transmit button on the headset. "Jack."

"I got you, Striker," Grimaldi called. "Sniper's at two o'clock, on top of the four-story building."

Bolan rolled into position, brought the M-16 to his shoulder and peered through the open sights.

The sniper was a head-and-shoulders silhouette against the bright sky on the building's roof.

He flicked the selector to single-fire, then squeezed off six deliberate rounds. More autofire raked the overturned car, then the sniper jerked and fell out of sight.

More Scuds filled the air. The explosions became a drumroll striking the city. Bolan saw two of them explode overhead and knew the UN forces had unleashed return fire from the Patriot systems set up at the temporary camp on the east side of the city. Debris continued to rain down around them from the stricken buildings ringing the street.

Without warning, the ground vibrations increased as a tank smashed through a small shop less than thirty yards away. The Executioner identified the tank as a British-made Challenger Main Battle Tank. A small, blue UN flag flew from the rear deck.

It finished smashing through the shop, massive treads churning, then crunched up onto an abandoned minivan sitting on rims. When the turret came around with a whir of servo motors loud enough to be heard over the crash and thunder of the bombing,

Bolan knew the tank was no longer under either British or UN control.

Talia Alireza fired at a black-cammied figure that threw itself to ground across the street.

"Come on!" Bolan yelled as he grabbed the woman by the arm and jerked her into motion. She started to resist, then went with him. Behind them, the tank's 120 mm turret gun fired a round into the minivan.

Bolan caught a glimpse of the vehicle leaping from the ground and turning cartwheels as it flew through the air. Then the concussed air caught up to him and the woman and slammed them into the ground. He hit the pavement with bruising impact, and heard the turret groan as it swiveled to fire again.

*   *   *   *   *

*The heart-stopping action continues
in the second book of The Storm Trilogy:*
Eye of the Storm, *coming in May.*